The Crezchek Files

Opening Statement

*Mr. Segally
Thanks for being
a trooper.
A very Merry Christmas!
Happy Readings & God bless...*

Dragica Lord
'2011

Dragica Lord

The Crezchek Files is a work of fiction. Names, characters and events are the imagination of the author and have been fabricated to fit the story. Any similarity to actual events or persons, living or dead, is entirely coincidental.

ISBN-978-0-615-50496-4

The Crezchek Files will be available in soft cover and

e-book

Published in the United States

I want to thank God for making this all happen.

Thank you Lord...

Acknowledgments

To the love of my life; my son, River Ellis Ludwig.
Without you, I don't know what my life would be like.
I love you so much more over, buddy.

Love, Mommy...

To the other love of my life; my husband, Kenny Ellis Ludwig. You are always there for me supporting me in whatever I want or need to do. For this, I thank you and I love you very much.

Love, your wife...Dragica

I want to thank all of my friends, new and old, for all of your support. All of you have been so wonderful during this process of creating "The Crezchek Files."

Thank you my friends...

I want to thank my friend, Stephanie Kincaid-editor. I appreciate all of your help and your words of encouragement. Your honesty and support out flowers a rose.

Thank you my friend...

Preamble

This court trial was written from a manuscript that just happened to be found after it was closed and misplaced some seventeen years ago. Even though the wording may be different it all means just the same.

After researching all the information that came from within the manuscript and all the questioning of potential witnesses, attorneys and two magistrates and after the courts announced a new trial was I then given the okay to begin to compose 'The Crezchek Files' into book form.   There are several names that arise in this book that have been changed to a certain degree of fictional character. It was of vital importance to protect both the innocent and the guilty parties in this case!

I have been sworn into secrecy, promising not to disclose any of the events, details, people or graphics, in any shape or form, relating to this case. The privacy act 113-CJD has been signed and dated on this day, February 16th, 2011, by Dragica Lord. The witness to this signing was before Magistrate Jean F. Howard of Gary, Indiana.

During my interviews with all these individuals associated with this case, I knew that I had to maintain extreme discretion with each of them. I had to be very careful with my wording and actions as I questioned them. There is so much more to this case than meets the eye.

The different dates, whether in correct order or not, that are mentioned here are the only dates that I was permitted to use at this time.

Due to privacy laws and the judicial system's protection of the rights of the American people, I was not allowed to disclose certain information. But what I was approved to reproduce is presented here for your examination.

Factual Information

Gary is a city in Lake County Indiana in the United States. It was established in 1906 by the Indigo Steel Corporation. The city was named after the lawyer and found chairperson of Indigo Steel, Albert, H. Gary.

Years ago most people left the city due to unemployment. There were 85% of the people who had gotten laid off losing their jobs and then many of the population of Gary started using and trading in illegal drugs.

After a three term democratic position Mayor Lewis King resigned from office on March of 2003, itching a desire to return to private law practice. Then on April 2, 1971, local officials chose former Lake County Commissioner and King rival Rudolph Clayton, to fill the remaining 21 of Kings term.

In March of 1972, the chief of police, deputy chief and a police sergeant were all indicted by the federal court for violating the civil rights of a Gary resident, a member of the Crezchek family!

There are different territory's within the City of Gary, Indiana:

Black Oak is the only primary white neighborhood in Gary. There were hundreds of fatalities found buried in one particular junk yard, Rayburn's, which is located on the west end of town. There were 47% of the bodies that were identified, 53% still remain as missing persons.

Ivanhoe was a housing project located on Gary's west

side along 13th avenue, east of Chase Street. It was closed in the summer of 1969, the facility was sealed off by a circular steel chain linked fence. The surrounding neighborhood has been noted as amongst the very worst 'ghettos' in America, compared to the Bronx in New York or Chicago's 'Wild 100's'.

Brunswick Park, along with five other surrounding recreational parks are all in the county located within the city limits of Gary. These parks play a big role in multiple murder cases which are unsolved and left in the file cabinet.

In the adjoining area, the housing market is so weak there right now you might as well buy in Ogden Dunes, It's five times better than the Miller section.

In the Aetna section of Gary, the highway at 12 and 20 is a round about big subdivision. Aetna is pretty much dilapidated all around. There is not a pleasant word to say about it. It is a very poor area which is a larger indicator than race. A lot of potholes in the roads, wild grass, shacks and 12 year olds taking over.

There have been many fatalities recovered in this area. A mass of white people moved during the 'white fight' back in the 50s. The majority of crimes in Gary are poor blacks on other poor blacks.

Gary itself just doesn't happened unless you are involved in drugs, which is the game changer here but if you work full-time, live back up in the hills by the beach, mind your own business, then nothing will happen to you, you are pretty safe there.

 The Crezchek family was rooted on the south west side of Gary, Indiana, in a part of the city by the name of Glen Park. The family grew up in the days of old. The older generation of the family grew up during the great depression and the baby boomers lived in poverty times. They were known to be a racial family until they started to immerse into politics. Then the family began to marry outside the black race into the white race of politicians.

Since the 1800s of the Crezchek family's existence, they either had alcoholism or drug addiction that ran in the family. Some family members were institutionalized for depression. Medical records indicated that abuse to family members goes back as far as doctors could remember.

They tried to keep this hush-hush!

Child Abuse is more than bruises and broken bones. Although physical abuse might be the most visible sign, other types of abuse, such as emotional or child neglect, also leave deep, long lasting scars.

Some signs of child abuse are sensitively complex and misunderstood, some more than others. However, by educating yourself on common types of abuse and what you can do about it, you can make a huge difference in a child's life. The earlier children who are abused get help, the greater chance they will have to heal from the abuse and not perpetuate the cycle.

Learn what the signs and symptoms of child abuse are and help break the pattern. Try to find out where to get help for these children and their caregivers. Children who have been abused for most of their life who have not gotten the proper help tend to either get into prostitution, drugs, gangs and even commit murder because of their past childhood abuse.

One of the most painful repercussions of child abuse is its tendency to repair itself.

Sadly but true, this is where it all began with the Crezchek family...

Opening Statement

PRESIDING JUDGE CHEDISTER: Mr. Brumenthal, you may begin with your opening statement.

MR. BRUMENTHAL: Thank you, Your Honor.

Ladies and Gentlemen of the Jury;

In 1973, the State of Indiana closed the Crezchek files. The out come of the murder case was due to insufficient evidence of the murders. There was a big outcry from the city's public, and the people of the city protested in front of the town hall.

They thought maybe, just maybe, they could be heard, but that wasn't the situation in these homicide proceedings.

The people of Gary, Indiana, wanted nothing but justice for the murder victims. The victims ranged in age from thirty-one to forty-eight years old.

All the victims were of both races, white and black.

All the carnage took place in the same town!

All the innocent fatalities were helpless human beings who didn't stand a chance at defending themselves. They had no idea that the day they were all viciously killed would be their last day here on earth. Their family members didn't even get to say goodbye. They didn't know that would be the last day they would ever see their loved ones for the last time.

The slaughterer had caused so much chaos in the town of Gary, Indiana, which almost caused the townspeople to banish from their once was a beautiful city to live in.

Gary, Indiana, is now the number one crime capital of the Unite States. There are approximately two to three homicides weekly—too many for the town's population. The percentage of abandoned homes has climbed up the scale to seventy-seven percent.

Ninety-two percent of all the homes that remain in the city are rat infested, and filthy and ready for condemnation. The living conditions in the town are nothing but pure surreal disgust. The black race population in Gary outweighs by far the white population race to almost nothing.

Gary, Indiana, is not, home sweet home, nor is it a place that can light a person's face. The decent people are all exiting the city and leaving behind all the memories that were once proud to become a memory.

Local authorities blame the high crime rate on nearby Chicago's drug influence as that city tears down public housing projects. Chicago has the reputation for being the Godfather to all surrounding cities and towns, especially Gary, Indiana. Chicago has set up their base of criminal gangsters to spread them out in the high crime areas such as Gary.

The murder rate in Gary, Indiana is 9.75 times the national average, and from year to year, the rate keeps going up. Who would have thought that 40 years ago, that Gary, Indiana, would now be a drug-infested murderous city?

So how did the city of Gary disturb the mind of a little boy who was born to a white mother and a black father who both made abusing drugs and alcohol an everyday part of their life?

The little boy who has adapted his whole life and lived on both sides of his family; the little boy who has been to eight different schools and kicked out of four and had been to another four moving all around, the little boy who has lived with other people more than his own mother and father.

As a little boy Anthony Crezchek was kept isolated from everything and everyone. He didn't even get the chance to experience life itself. The day he was born, is when the abuse first started. He was always put in the crib to cry himself to sleep. He had nobody to hold him or rock him or even to sing him a lullaby or to just say, "Good night" or "I love you." He was cut off from all forms and acts of life and he wasn't allowed to have friends or even hang out with his own cousins.

Mr. Crezchek suffered severely from child abuse his entire childhood. Child abuse is harm to, or neglect of, a child by another person, whether it be adult or child. Child abuse does happens in all cultural, ethnic, and income groups. Child abuse can be physical, emotional, verbal, sexual or through neglect. Abuse can cause serious injury to the child and may even result in death.

In this case, Mr. Crezchek miraculously survived all the unspeakable acts of abuse inflicted upon his mind and body, and the fact that he maintained the will to stay alive is a miracle in itself. The percentage of anyone at all to have lived through all the shocking and terrorizing experiences as Mr. Crezchek had to face throughout his whole life has risen up to perhaps 67 percent.

The time spent home with his parents had become a sickening grossly abusive situation which back then so many years ago others wouldn't even think about getting involved.

So in this case, in this little boys mind, everything kept building and building up until one day he just couldn't take it any more. The flashbacks of his childhood overrode the good memories that were to be made. The little boy was not at fault for his unhappy life that he has lead. He is not responsible for the thoughts and actions his mind created from his childhood.

This young man who sits before all of you in this courtroom today has been mentally disturbed. He has been savagely beaten and raped repeatedly over and over again. He has been burnt on different parts of his body with cigarettes so very badly that his skin has indentations and his skin scarred blackened with color.

This young man when only an infant, 18 months old, is a matter of fact—was punched and socked in his stomach until he could barely get up and walk. Doctors have stated that at such a young age, at 18 months old, the infant is very lucky to be alive and that not many could survive that type of beating.

The drugs and alcohol had eaten up the minds of Mr. Crezchek's parents to the point that they could not even bathe themselves. At the age of seven, Mr. Crezchek had to run bathwater for both his parents and bathe not only his father, but his mother as well. The little boy was treated as a slave had been in the days of slavery. He knew nothing else but to serve and wait on others; he never got the opportunity to be a kid and run and play and have fun.

Mr. Crezchek has never even cracked a smile on his once-oval-shaped child's face until the day he was freed.

The little boy who lived inside the body of Mr. Crezchek, went hungry for days on end, without any food whatsoever. This little boy had no choice but to go to the grocery store and steal food so that he would not starve to death. He never knew where his next meal was coming from. He suffered from malnutrition on numerous occasions. His little body was three times smaller than what it should have been.

Yeah, that's right: when Anthony Crezchek was only eight years old, his little torso resembled that of a five year old. His body was not growing to the proper height or weight for his age.

He has stated that on more than one occasion, he groped through the dumpsters outside of stores and restaurants instead of stealing. His stomach was so pained by starvation that he really didn't care where his next meal came from.

Unfortunately, that wasn't the only horrific event that would take place in his past childhood.

Mr. Crezchek has not only had his body sold for sexual favors to strangers but has `been exposed to his only aunt he thought he could trust. He found out differently one day when the aunt, Mrs. Murdock, came calling at the house to deliver drugs to his parents when they could not pay with green money. She grazed the boy over and simply told them that the boy would do. The parents went into the other room as if nobody else were there with them.

Thinking she, the aunt was going to rescue him from these surroundings but only to find out she had other plans for him was another low blow to his trusted eight-year-old mind. Mrs. Murdock told the boy to go downstairs where she then made sexual contact with him.

A neighbor, who wishes to remain anonymous, states she had seen the boy run from the basement door on numerous occasions and that you could just tell that something was not right by the look on his face.

Both of his parents were at fault for prostituting his body in exchange for drugs. The boy was kept for days on end by his rapist who had become his *John* and only knew of this behavior to be a part of his life. The little boy was not allowed to go outside unless picked up by a titz and returned within thirty minutes after leaving.

When Mr. Crezchek was just eleven years old he by that time had just enough of all the mortifying and degrading abuse his mind and body could hold.

So now we ask; why were these murders covered up and who were they covered up by? Charges have been brought up against Mr. Crezchek for what reason? Is it possible that Mr. Crezchek is not the guilty party in this case at all? Why has the courts waited until now to reopen this case some seventeen years later? Why has the community of Gary, Indiana, failed to comply with the court orders?

This is the third time this case has been opened with the intent to place blame on Mr. Crezchek. The last two times this case was reopened it was believed that the surrounding area of politicians were in one hell of a mess. It was thought best to get it covered up quickly so they pointed their dirty fingers back at Mr. Crezchek.

Why not! This particular case has been opened and closed according to the court system for certain reasons that were not disclosed to the public in open court. It was said that it was not mandatory to bring other accusations other than this case to the table. It was said that only one case should be tried at a time.

There seems to be various missing and untold pages to this story.

All the evidence that would have brought this hard cold case to justice has disappeared mysteriously, and there is not a single soul alive who knows what happened to it. The only link that would close this book *is* the missing evidence.

There are issues that have been brought to the attention of one of the in-house politicians who at this time request to be silent in this case until the time of subpoena. Has this court case been politically tampered with by certain parties of the Gary government? If this is the case that there is corruption going on within the city of the Gary Government then what is the connection with the Crezchek family?

The Crezchek files have been a hush-hush situation for seventeen years now and evidently there has been some kind of information that has been leaked out of the secretive circle and made it to be the fault of Anthony Crezchek.

The court is now contemplating at this time if

Anthony Crezchek will be allowed to testify on his own behalf. If the court finds that he will not hurt himself by sitting on the witness stand then Mr. Crezchek will be allowed to take the stand later in this trial.

As a little boy, Anthony Crezchek dealt with so much turmoil, heartache and so much grief in his life, so much more than a little boy should have had to.

One question that arises comes to mind is why didn't anyone at all try to help this little boy? Are all the people of Gary, Indiana, that disturbed?

You would think that someone would at least drop a letter or anonymous call to the police department, but nothing. People in that town just didn't want to get involved.

There have been so many people heart stricken by these events but for every reason imaginable, Anthony Crezchek has been dragged back, not once, not twice, but three times, into court for the same allegations. He has not ever been charged with any of these said murders. So why is he then being accused of his family's murders and tried in these proceedings after seventeen years?

We are here to prove to you that Anthony Crezchek is innocent and did not because of all the evil put upon him act out any killings on any of his own family members whatsoever.

With that said;

On different dates all within the same year, December 19th, February 3rd, and 7th, and April 27th, 1971, seven people were murdered. There are unknown reasons as to why all these murders took place.

All the witnesses in the 1973 court session testified that every single victim that had their life taken were helpless human beings just trying to make a living as you or I. Not one of them had any sort of record and were very highly talked about and respected by others who knew of them in the community, so says the defense.

Then why did they all become victims? How could they all be respected if they were all the abuser of Anthony Crezchek?

Well, we have just recently discovered that every witness who had testified in the 1973 court session testified falsely under oath. There has been another witness that has come forward with this information claiming to be present on numerous occasions during the secretive circle meetings when these witnesses were offered money to carry out this act on this one day in court.

All the people who had participated in the aforementioned action were later subpoenaed by the court and ordered to go into the judge's chambers where they were to be questioned and interrogated on separate occasions. All these people were charged with perjury and served time in jail for their unlawful actions.

The witness will remain silent at this time.

The Murders

12-19-1971

On the night of December 19th, 1971, a double homicide took place right before the Christmas holiday. The parents of Anthony Crezchek had both been sadistically murdered.

The father, Chris Crezchek, age 39, was found in the bathroom sitting on the toilet seat, slouched over against the wall. Each one of his digits had been cut off.

It was clear that both of his hands were

placed on the bathroom sink, and all fingers were chopped off with an extremely sharp blade of some sort and done with an exceptionally clean cut.

The victim's fingers to this day remain unfound. His scalp at the hairline was scraped off to the bare skull and pulled back down to his neck and left hanging there. His neck was slit with a metal can lid and sitting there on the floor of the bathroom was an empty corn can filled with his blood. Tied around his arm was a bandana which you could obviously see that it had a missing part that had been torn off. The cause of death; the victim bled to death.

The mother, Latisha Crezchek, age 38, was found sitting up in a chair in the living room. Her nostrils were slit with a razor blade. On her left forearm, apparently, the skin had been cut into about an inch deep and inside the wound, the coroner found a bag containing the drug, heroin.

This victim also took a gunshot to the inside of her left eardrum. It looked as if the gun was placed inside her ear and then the trigger was pulled. The cause of death; gunshot wound to the head.

The victims apparently died within just minutes of each other. The city's coroner stated that the homicides could not have been committed by only one person. The way the victims were killed indicated that multiple people had participated in these ruthless and grotesque killings.

At the time of these killings Anthony Crezchek was seventeen years old and had been living in Detroit Michigan concentrating on making a new life for himself. He thought if he had moved to another state that he would be far enough away from his dreadful past and could try to rebuild a life he never has had.

But regrettably, because of all the misfortune of the cities corruption that had been formed within the Gary government, Anthony Crezchek's life is once again now disturbed and turned upside down.

02-03-1971

On February 3rd, 1971, a single homicide was committed. The victim Allen Crezchek, 48, was murdered. Allen Crezchek was a brother to Chris Crezchek who also was an uncle to Anthony Crezchek, the accused in this case.

On this 3rd day of February, the time of death was announced at 3:32 a.m. in the early morning hour. The Lake County Coroner Jack White conducted an autopsy on this victim on February 4, 1971. The autopsy was performed by three pathologists; Jack

White, Doris Remling and Jerald Wiston.

The victim Allen Crezchek was found by one of his acquaintances two days later, after his death. He was found in his bedroom lying on the bed without any clothes on his body, his left arm with a rubber hose tied around it and a syringe lying next to his beginning stage of decomposed body.

The Coroner stated that the syringe was filled with pure heroin and that there was enough heroin in that syringe to kill five people. The cause of death; heroin over dose.

02-07-1971

On February 7th, 1971, a triple homicide occurred in the Glen Park area of Gary. On the block of 42nd and Delaware Street, gunshots were heard by neighbors who did not want to be identified.

The police were called to the crime scene in the early evening hour of 8:23 p.m. The home was a known drug house. A drug house is a home that druggies go to get high. When the police arrived at the crime scene only the three dead bodies were to be found.

Among the dead were; Bobby Crezchek, 39, Michael

Crezchek, 41 and Erin Crezchek, 44, all of Gary. All three victims were brothers of Chris Crezchek and the uncles of Anthony Crezchek, the accused in this case.

Neighbors told police that they had seen eight gang members get out of a blue van. Two went to the back of the house and two remained in front of the house and four went inside the house. Once the gang members were inside of the house there were four people, druggies, which left the premises.

The neighbors reported hearing arguing going on in the drug house and gunshots fired and then there was a sudden silence.

The gang members then left the location in Glen Park. Neighbors said that they have never seen the blue van before in the neighborhood.

All three victims were shot execution style. Execution style is where the victims are told to kneel down on the floor with their hands behind their backs and then shot in the back of the head.

One of the victims, Erin Crezchek had taken a hard blow to the right side of his head in the temple area. His eye was swollen and discolored. No weapons or evidence were found at the crime scene. The cause of death for all three victims: Gun shot by execution style.

There was an investigation done by Gary Detective, Art Bruder. He stated that the Crezchek family has been almost all wiped out. Detective Bruder says that he believed definitely that there was some kind of a connection between the gang in Gary and the Crezchek family. The blue van that was recognized by a neighbor to this day has never been seen again.

04-27-1971

On April 27[th,] 1971, Lena Murdock, the sister of Chris Crezchek also the aunt of Anthony Crezchek was found dead in her car on 2nd Avenue and Broadway in Gary.

Police were called to the scene of the crime when a motorist was on their way to work and came to a stoplight on the corner of 2nd and Broadway. As their vehicle came to a standstill at the intersection there was one car ahead of them and it was not moving. They continued to go around the vehicle but as they approached its side, they realized something was wrong when they seen Mrs. Murdock's head facing toward the outside of the driver's side of the car. The motorist honked the horn thinking that Mrs. Murdock had fallen asleep, but when she didn't move at all, the motorist called for help. The body was found at 6:23 a.m.

Detective Art Bruder stated that the victim Mrs. Murdock was found with a cord wrapped around her neck. Detective Bruder said that the assailant had to be in the back seat of her car and then strangled her from behind. The cause of death: Death by strangulation.

There were seven people murdered on four different occasions. All seven victims were related to Anthony Crezchek, the accused in this trial.

Why has Anthony Crezchek's family all been murdered? Well, that is why we are here today to prove that Anthony Crezchek who stands one more time on trial did not maliciously kill his family.

The prosecution side is pointing their finger at

Anthony Crezchek. And why? It appears that we are also here today to prove that these murders that took place all revolved around the political group in Northwest Indiana, Gary!

In two of the homicides that were committed we believe that the Cryp gangsters of Gary had some kind of involvement, but there has been no evidence to be found as of yet.

Without the evidence we can not use it against the Cryps at this time!

But just because of all the bad history of the gang and its violence.,we are directing all possible fault towards them.

On Tyler Street and 3rd Avenue in the Aetna section of Gary, Indiana, where the Crezchek family resided also resided the Cryp gangsters.

The Aetna section is located on Gary's far east side along the Dunes highway. Aetna predates the city of Gary. It was a company town that was founded in 1881 by the Easton Powder Works, an explosion company, which closed with the end of world war 1. It has been said that the Cryps have taken that section of Gary over as their territory.

The town of Aetna was annexed in 1928 around the same time Gary annexed the town of Miller. The eastern edge of Aetna is complete wilderness where there have been numerous fatalities uncovered.

The Aetna section of Gary is not a safe place to raise a family. Shootings and drug deals are all surreal. Racism is very much a happening thing there. There are better choices than East Gary for safe 'family friend' living.

Be prepared to see gang rise against gang everywhere you go in that section of Gary. The Cryps do a lot of socializing in that town.

The Cryps gangsters are a largely African-American Chicago-based Street gang which has, over the years, grown into one of the largest criminal organizations in the United States, known to be involved in about $100 million a year of drug trafficking. They are well-known to be one of the biggest Drug Lords around the Northwest Indiana and Chicago land area. They are also known for wearing skull cap bandanas when they are being initiated in order to get into the gang.

It is believed to be that at least two of the murders may be linked to the Cryp gangsters. After conducting an autopsy and a further investigation, Gary's Coroner, Jack White, contacted Detective Art Bruder who worked for the Gary Police Department and explained to him that the bandana that was tied around the arm of one of the murdered victims matched the skull bandanas used in the gang's initiation rituals.

Bruder then conducted a further investigation into the gang. A DNA test will be performed on the skull cap bandana and then the search for the gangster that will match the exact DNA. The DNA test will tell us if it matches one of the gang members by the sweat that was on the bandana, that is, only if the right gang member were to be found. And that would be like finding a needle in a haystack.

So now we know—or we are presuming— that the Cryps had some kind of link to these two homicides on December 19th, 1971, but just not a sufficient amount of evidence to prove any one party guilty.

Detective Bruder investigated the gang but could not make any arrests at that time. He was told by the states attorney, Marcus Debroy, to drop the investigation of the bandana; for what reasons are still left unknown.

Witness Questioning

Using common sense and looking into and finding other drug addicted people who had in the past indeed purchased their sweet medicine from the Cryps, these people will be silent witnesses for fear of their lives that the Cryps will hunt them down and violate them. Remember that the Cryps have no mercy upon ones soul for whatever it may be! Or at least that is what the public made their reputation out to look like.

On the first day of questioning the first silent witness, the witness admitted buying drugs. Heroin was the drug purchased from the gang from this witness.

Witness substantiated that they have crossed paths with Latisha Crezchek on quite a few occasions coming and going to make a drug deal. Witness also confirmed that the drug deal was indeed made with the Cryp gangsters of Gary, Indiana.

When trust is secured between the Cryps and the drug buyer, the Cryps chooses one of their newly initiated gang members to make house calls.

During this process of delivering the drugs there are at least five gangsters close by within harms reach. Three of the gang members would enter the house and two would remain outside—one in front of the house and one in the rear of the house. The three gang members on the inside of the house, they all take standing positions four-in-half feet from one another.

Before the gang members arrive at the drug buyer's house they, meaning the person buying the drug, they are instructed to leave the money inside a shoe and place the shoe by the front door. The drug buyer is then to exit the room and not to return until they hear a gang member cough two times before walking out the door.

By the drug deal being made this way, this ensures that there are not any witnesses to the deal. The Cryp gangsters are known to take every precaution they can.

The witness says that they themselves claimed to have been in the Crezchek house at the time the Cryps were there, but the witness was asked to leave.

We now know that there is without a doubt some type of link between the Crezchek family and the Cryp gangsters, but just not enough evidence, if any, to charge the Cryps with premeditated murder. But for all we know it just may be drug related.

The second witness agreed to be an informant for the FBI; subject to being accepted into the Federal Witness Security Program. This person is a very crucial witness and their testimony will put them in immediate danger if not accepted into the program.

The courts are awaiting The U.S. Attorney General's office, which has the final word on the admission of this witness into the program. Therefore, the second witness will be excused from testifying in court at this time until further notice.

Another witness has come forward from the Baptist Church of God in Gary, Indiana. This witness is a pastor of the Baptist Church and agreed to testify on the behalf of Anthony Crezchek. This witnesses name is Pastor Francis Jackson.

Pastor Jackson has been serving the Baptist Church for 22 years and says that he will testify on the behalf of Anthony Crezchek that he has not committed any of these cold-blooded murders. Pastor Jackson first met the accused when Anthony Crezchek was a little boy.

He first noticed the little boy one Sunday morning when he was preaching his sermon. He noticed that in one corner of the church the little boy was standing all by himself with a lost look written all over his face. After the church services were over, the pastor attempted to approach the child but he sped out the door.

Pastor Jackson said that the little boy seemed fearful of him so he did not continue the confrontation. Pastor Jackson stated that the little boy attended the church the following Sunday and every Sunday from then on out. It wasn't until almost a year later that Anthony opened up to him and let him into his miserable and depressed childhood life. Pastor Jackson stated that he was shocked by what this boy has had to go through. He said that he has never seen anyone suffer the severity of abuse that Anthony Crezchek received from his abusers. Anthony Crezchek was not abused by just his mother and father but by the entire side of the Crezchek family.

As a victim, he has received sexual, physical and mental abuse and that is why we are here to prove today that just because Anthony Crezchek was the soul survivor of his family does not mean that the seven Crezchek murders that took place were committed by him. All of Anthony's relatives on his father's side have been killed. What would have made someone do these horrific and revolting murders?

The other side, the prosecution side has pointed their fingers at Anthony Crezchek because of his past abusive childhood.

If this is the case, he would have to be just as insane as his family members who had abused him in the first place. Pastor Jackson was just outraged with the Crezchek family. Anthony Crezchek started going to meet with Pastor Jackson almost two to three times a week seeking comfort from the church. He said that the little boy, at that time, Anthony, wanted to know how to let God into his life. The pastor was taken aback by the little boy who has been so abused by so many different people and yet he somehow found the strength to let God into his wretched heart.

There were many nights that Anthony would stay in a little room on a single cot in the church without his parents even knowing he was gone out of the home. About the same time he was being outputted by his john for sexual favors is the time that Anthony had found God. Is a matter of fact, Anthony was running away one Sunday morning from the sick man who was pimping him out to any gender, any person that would pay a dollar.

Pastor Jackson states that he wanted to notify police but Anthony pleaded with him not to because he said that he did not want his parents taken away from him.

Imagine that, ladies and gentlemen! Despite all the abuse the little boy took he still found it in his heart to have love for his parents no matter what.

In March of 1962, Pastor Jackson clearly remembers one late night Monday evening Anthony had knocked on the door and when Pastor Jackson opened the door the little boy was standing outside in the rain with hardly any clothes on. Pastor Jackson states that when he got the little boy inside and dried him off he could see burns on his skinny forearms and burn marks on his legs and even burns on his buttocks. He tried once again to notify the authorities but Anthony pleaded with him again and again not to.

Pastor Jackson states that the both of them, he the pastor and the accused Anthony Crezchek has many a night prayed and cried for God's help for this family.

One day, Pastor Jackson clearly remembers

that he went to the Crezchek family's home and asked Anthony's parents to find it in their hearts to let the little boy go and live with the Pastor at the church. Both the parents refused the offer stating that Anthony's place was at home, that what kind of parents they would be if they let him go live elsewhere. Picture that!

He recalls that the house was so filthy and the smell was later to be found as the drug, heroin. The living conditions were so unsuitable for any person at all to live in. The floor probably hadn't been swept for years and the furniture was practically all fallen apart and on the floor. There were cock roaches and ants everywhere. "How someone could live like that, I don't know," stated Pastor Jackson. "It's a wonder the health department doesn't condemn the house and tear it down."

In March of 1962, Only three days after the fact of trying to persuade the Crezchek family to let Anthony live with him at the church, Pastor Jackson had not heard from Anthony and the Pastor grew worried. He decided to go over to the Crezchek house around 8:30 in the evening. He knocked on the front door of the house and no answer. He then proceeded to go to the back of the house and knocked on the back door, still there was no answer. He could sense something was not right. His gut feeling told him something was wrong. He opened the door and entered the house through the kitchen where he then walked into the living area only to find both the parents of Anthony Crezchek, the father sitting on the couch and the mother kneeling on the floor next to him. The mother, Latisha Crezchek, had rubber tubing wrapped around her upper arm with the end in her mouth biting down on it. Chris Crezchek, the father, was holding a syringe with the needle in her arm.

Both the parents of Anthony Crezchek were exceedingly high that they didn't even notice the pastor was in the house. The pastor walked down the hallway checking every room hoping to find the little boy, Anthony. No luck upstairs, so he had a feeling of uncertainty rumble through his body as he approached the kitchen. The basement door was slightly ajar and a child's cry of pain and agony was trailing up the stairs. Not knowing what to expect, he then made his way to the cracked opened door of the basement. He began stepping down the stairs one by one until he reached the bottom stair. The little boy, Anthony Crezchek, was lying on the floor of the basement about five feet away from the staircase.

He seen the boy lying on the floor curled up against the wall. Pastor Jackson picked him up and carried him out the back door. Anthony Crezchek's parents didn't even know he had left the home. After they entered the church is when he realized that Anthony had been beaten once again.

Pastor Jackson just could not understand how the Crezchek family savagely and appallingly abused him. This little boy amazingly suffered abuse through not only his entire infant and toddler years, but most of his teen life as well.

Mayor

In the spring of 1968, shit hit the fan in Gary, Indiana. Mayor Rick Hatcher made a mistake on his behalf and was found to be a member of the secretive circle that had been formed back in the year 1957.

Mayor Hatcher was charged by the city of the Gary courts for corruption within the government rules of Gary. There were charges brought up against him one after another. The charges brought up against Mayor Hatcher are as follows; having sexual relations with a minor, money racketeering, mishandling of court files and drug abuse.

All four charges filed against Mayor Hatcher were later dropped by the city of the Gary government when things calmed down and the people of Gary were no longer talking about the corruption that had erupted. Mayor Hatcher was also charged a short time later with bamboozling the Gary police department.

According to Mayor Hatcher when he testified in court, he said that homicides are hard to predict and therefore are hard to prevent.

But you know as well as I do, ladies and gentlemen of this court, that without enough honest law enforcement out there trying to protect the people of Gary, these notorious and heinous crimes are just not going to stop!

Since Mayor Rick Hatcher has been in office in Gary, Indiana, the police force was stricken with a pay cut and the overtime slashed to almost nothing.

There are two-thirds of the police department who sit at a desk with a higher rank of authority while one-third is left working on the streets.

The gangs that rise against gangs are more

than half the cities population, so without ample law enforcement how can the city of Gary, Indiana, be controlled and a safe community to live in.

It was proven beyond a reasonable doubt that Mayor Rick Hatcher had lessened the protection for the city of Gary, Indiana, and had kept the money for himself with depositing the money into a bank account in the state of Ohio. So for the cause of endangering the city of Gary, Indiana's community, Mayor Rick Hatcher was relieved of his duty as mayor of Gary, Indiana.

Mayor Hatcher was also seen in the neighborhood on the early morning of April 27th, 1971, close by the old Goldblatt's building where Lena Murdock was murdered. He has been interrogated on more than one occasion by the CIA, but Hatcher will not change his story.

The CIA when investigating, did find out that he, Rick Hatcher, was somehow related to the Crezchek family. We will later find out how and whom he was related to in the Crezchek family from the testimony of one of the most vital witnesses in this trial.

Crucial Witness

We have brought to you, ladies and gentlemen of this court, the most crucial witness, whose testimony is the most imperative you will hear in this case. This witness has been serving as a police officer in a Northwest Indiana police department as one of their high ranking officials. This witness has come forth and has agreed to testify and turn states evidence not only against the Cryp gangsters, but the Major of Gary, the FBI and the Gary government officials—only if absolutely necessarily needed!

The witness here has completed an unbelievable amount of heroism throughout his life with not only trying to keep adults in line but also has done amazingly work with kids and teens.

In exchange for his testimony, the courts has agreed to grant an acquittal and place him under the states protection for his own behalf. This witnesses name will be inaccessible.

Let the record show that the other witness who was a magistrate of the court had been subpoenaed would not come forth with any information and was given a jail sentence for failing to comply with the court orders.

Jamie's Statement

Detective Art Bruder the investigating officer in this case was told on different occasions to drop and walk away from these murder allegations by Gary's Chief of Police, Marcus Debroy. Chief Debroy denied any such allegations.

Detective Bruder was, at a later date, contacted by the CIA out of Boston, Massachusetts, to cooperate with their investigation of the Crezchek files. The CIA had questioned the detective and interrogated him for hours about the Crezchek investigation.

Before the interrogation with the CIA, Detective Bruder was grilled by the FBI and the subject of a letter had come up several times. Detective Bruder stated that he told FBI that he had no recollection of anything being said about a letter. He also stated that the FBI Agent Scott Preswood indicated to Detective Bruder to expunge the meeting that happened between him and FBI. Agent Preswood suggested that maybe detective Bruder should reason with him but Detective Bruder said there was no reasoning about anything. He was then instructed once again to eradicate that meeting before he got to his car. He was then told to leave the building.

From the time he left the FBI building to the time he returned to the Gary Police Department he was told that there were charges being brought against him and that he needed to hand in his gun and badge.

In June of 1968, Detective Art Bruder was

placed in handcuffs and thrown in jail. There were no phone calls to be made to his wife until the next midmorning. Mrs. Arlene Bruder, Detective Art Bruder's spouse, was notified by phone at approximately 10:48 a.m. which she then contacted her Attorney, Kent Sealander. Mr. Sealander went to bail Detective Bruder out of the Gary jailhouse complex at 11:29 a.m. Attorney Sealander was told by Chief Marcus Debroy that Detective Art Bruder had been charged with tampering with court files. Chief Debroy stated that a former employee of the Gary Government complex who had worked in the courts department had seen Detective Bruder go into the file room and take out files from the cabinet. This unknown witness, has without any explanation, disappeared after her testimony and no longer is employed at the government complex of Gary, Indiana, and not to be found anywhere.

The courts are now in a debate at this time as to whether or not her testimony should be used in this case. There were no other witnesses who saw Detective Bruder take the files.

Detective Bruder stated that three weeks later,

he was contacted by phone by a young woman who sounded terrified, pleading with him to meet with her. She said that she needed his help, that she could not talk over the telephone, but that he should meet her at the club house of the Mansard Apartments in Griffith, a nearby town. He agreed to meet with her on that following day at mid morning at 8:30 a.m. sharp. He was told to go to the apartments across Ridge Road on the North side where she would be waiting for him in the club house.

The next morning, as Detective Bruder entered the club house, the door closed behind him. When he turned around there was a young lady that grabbed his hand and told him to follow her. The young lady led him down the hallway and into an office and closed the door behind them. Before Detective Bruder could say anything, a young man came out of the bathroom and introduced himself as having a connection to the Cryp gangsters from Gary. He called himself Jamie, AKA 'Snowman.'

This young man received this name from the head leader of the Cryps following one of his initiation tasks. For those of you who are not familiar with some of laymen terms, 'Snow' is a nickname for the illegal drugs cocaine and heroin, "man" is directed to the person who sells the drugs. Jamie stated that he knew for a fact that there was indeed cocaine and heroin being distributed by the Cryps. He was ordered by the lead gang member known as 'The King' to deliver cocaine and heroin to different dealers. He also told to Detective Bruder that he assisted in watching all the Crezchek murders take place.

In the month of September, 1971, Jamie Jackson was initiated into the Cryp gangsters of Gary, Indiana. After the initiation, he was instructed to attend one of the gangs in-house meetings in the old Jewish building downtown, on 3rd and Georgia. He was to arrive promptly on time at 1:15 p.m., enter through the alley entrance of the building and go downstairs.

During this meeting, the topic of the murders that were about to take place was discussed for future activities. Jamie was given orders to participate in these forthcoming events that were about to take place in the upcoming year. He was given a green hunting knife that was used to slit open and gut the stomach of deer once they were dead.

After the meeting, after this well-thought-out plan, Jamie was under the control of two other gang members who, when they left the building, took Jamie with them to another vacant building. They took him to an old abandoned home on 12th Place in the Aetna section of Gary. This particular abandoned home had a garage that was built into the side of a hill in the rear of the building.

The two gang members directed Jamie to go to the basement, and they followed him. As they neared the door they were about to enter, Jamie stated that there was such a fowl disgusting odor reaping in the air you could hardly help from not gagging, but they still entered the room. In the northwest corner of the room there sat a cabinet type of box that was approximately two feet in height by three feet wide.

Mr. Jackson, watched as the one gang member known as MJ unlocked and opened the cabinet door. MJ pulled out a cat that was about halfway dead and laid it on the top of the cabinet. He then told Jamie to stab the cat in the throat with the hunting knife he was given earlier that day.

Jackson said that he felt like puking his guts up but when he looked at the cat, the cat was in so much pain, all the yelping and crying it was doing, he just wanted to put the cat out of its misery. So he took the hunting knife out of his pants pocket and flipped it opened and grabbed the cat with his left hand while he raised the knife up in the air with his right hand and went down for the kill.

He said that the two other gang members seemed to really get a sick kick out of the kill and told Jamie he would have no problem come time for the planned activities to keep his knife sharpened and to be ready for that coming day.

The night before the first murder, the double homicide that was about to take place, Jamie was given notice by one of the gang members that one of the activity events would be in order for the next day, and that two gang members would be by to pick him up at 5:30 p.m. at the Hilltop.

The Hilltop was one of the old abandoned

buildings downtown Gary that the Cryps used for in-house meetings.

On the following day, December 19th, 1971, at just about 5:10 p.m., Jamie Jackson set out from his premises and went to the Hilltop to meet the other gang members.

When he arrived at the Hilltop, there were three other gang members along with the Cryps leader in the room. Jamie was ordered to sit down and listen and to 'listen good,' because there were no mistakes to be made that night. The gang leader gave out all the instructions that were to be followed by the members and Jamie, being a newly initiated member, was on the low bottom of the totem pole, which meant that he had the leftovers and had to do what the others did not.

The gangs leader, 'The King,' told Jamie that this would pave the way as to whether or not Jamie would show his true colors to the gang. He also warned Jamie that if there were any signs of betrayal from him in any way, he would have to suffer the consequences of the aftermath.

Jamie Jackson stated that at approximately 6:00 p.m. the meeting was over and MJ, Mojo, Truce and Jamie left the building. From the Hilltop, they made one more stop and that was to a nearby gas station. At the gas station, one of the gang members, Mojo, got out of the car they were driving and went straight over to the public pay telephone, where he then placed a call. Jamie said that he had no idea to whom the call was made. Mojo then got back into the car and confirmed that everything was set to go.

Jamie said that his heart fell to the ground and he wanted to get out, but he knew he could not. By this time, it was starting to get dark, and the driver of the car, MJ, drove with caution to their destination and parked the car just about a quarter of a block from Chris and Latisha Crezchek's home, the victims in this case.

All four, MJ, Mojo, Truce and Jamie got out of the car and Jamie stated that no sooner did they get out of the car that another gang member from out of the clear blue sky jumped into the drivers side and drove off.

Jamie's instructions were to follow behind Mojo, which meant he would be in front of Truce, who would be the last person to enter the home. As they approached the victims' home, Jamie was instructed to go with MJ toward the rear of the home, while Truce and Mojo went around to the front.

Jamie and MJ were to wait until MJ's watch beeped to enter the home. Two minutes later, the watch went off, MJ nodded at Jamie and the two of them proceeded to enter the home. Jamie stated that as soon as they were inside the home, the other two gang members had already been inside and waiting close by the bathroom door for Chris Crezchek to come out.

As Chris Crezchek opened the bathroom door, Mojo barged in and pushed Chris Crezchek back into the bathroom. Truce then rushed in and grabbed him by the shirt and then sat him down on the toilet. Jamie said that Chris Crezchek was so high on heroin that he didn't seem to have really any kind of an inclination as to what was about to happen to him.

Mojo took his bandana off of his head and wrapped it tight around the mouth of the victim. Truce clutched on to Chris Crezchek's left hand, placing it on the bathroom sink and then reached into his front left side of his pants and pulled out a Buck knife.

Jamie stated that Truce then went down on Crezchek's fingers so fast that he barley caught what had happened. Mojo was behind Chris Crezchek holding onto him with his arms around his chest and then Truce grabbed him by the hair and put the knife to the top of his forehead and slit the top of his scalp and tore it back to the neck and left it hanging.

Jamie stated then that Mojo then took what looked like a thin round piece of metal and slit Crezchek's throat and placed a can of some sort on the floor to let the blood drip, then the bandana was torn in half and tied around his right arm.

Jamie Jackson said they shut the bathroom door and he was then indoctrinated to head in the direction of where Latisha Crezchek was in the living room.

MJ whispered into Jamie's ear, telling him to walk behind Latisha and wrap both arms tight around her chest, to hold her arms down to her side. MJ held her legs and feet.

Jamie stated that Truce had in his hand something that looked like a razor blade and sliced her nostrils.

He then took the Buck knife and cut into her forearm, and reached in with his fingers and took out a chunk of flesh. Mr. Jackson, Jamie, said that Latisha's eyes started to roll back and she was making a crying noise like a wild cat. MJ took out a gun and placed it in her ear and pulled the trigger. Then Truce put a little baggie of heroin into the hole that was cut in her arm.

Jamie Jackson stated that it all happened so fast and all he could see was blood that came from the victim, dripping from his eyebrows, at the time of the killing.

He also said that he never in his life had witnessed something so viciously morbid then what he had seen on that unforgettable night.

Unfortunately, that was not the only murder he had to witness and participate in; Jamie Jackson stated that the second murder that he had witnessed was that of the victim Allen Crezchek.

Mr. Jackson stated that on the early evening of this homicide, he was given the instructions on what was to take place and what his position in this activity would be.

Jackson was ordered on that evening to pick up the heroin from one of the gangs in house buildings, put it in a cigarette pack and keep it in his coat pocket. Then from there he was to go to meet up with JT at the Black Oak Tap on Calhoun and 25th Avenue.

He was told to go into the bar and sit on the second stool facing the bar at the end of the left side. He was to order a tequila sunrise, drink half and push the drink up to the edge. He was then to light a cigarette and place it in the ashtray and to keep facing forward no matter what he heard or felt.

Jamie said that someone came up behind him and said that it felt like someone went into his coat pocket. He stayed seated like he was instructed to do then Jackson got up two minutes later and left the bar. From there he was to meet up with JT.

Jamie got into his car and reached into his pocket only to find the cigarette pack which contained the heroin gone but in its place was a different cigarette pack. Inside the pack of cigarette box was a piece of paper in replacement of the drug. On the paper was an address along with the orders he was to follow. He was to go to Buy-Low, a local grocery store on 49th Avenue, leave his car and from there he was to be picked up by a 1971 green escort driven by JT at 12:00 a.m. sharp.

They drove to the location and JT parked the vehicle about a block from the victim's home. The two gang members got out of the car and walked down the alley way to the back of Allen Crezchek's home. That would be where they both entered through the back door of the home. Jackson followed JT to the back bedroom where Allen Crezchek was sitting up in his bed, looking like he had been out of it for days already.

JT told Jamie to go to the kitchen to get a glass of water and as he returned he could see JT and Allen Crezchek exchanging words. He said that JT's words escalated to a sharp toned voice which Allen Crezchek then reacted to just sitting there listening without saying another word. JT told Jamie to tie the rubber tubing around Allen Crezchek's arm then motioned him to move back. JT put a pair of latex gloves on and took out the heroin from his pant pocket and filled a syringe full with the drug. Jamie stated that within seconds the victim was already slouching over.

JT and Jackson then left the home.

The murder of Lena Murdock-Crezchek, the sister of Chris Crezchek and aunt of Anthony Crezchek was also witnessed and assisted by the man sitting here in this court room today.

Jackson stated that on the day of the murder, one of the gang members, Hennessy, dropped by his place and gave the orders for Lena Murdock's murder that was about to occur late that night, into the early morning hour.

Jamie was to meet Hennessy on the corner of 4th Avenue and Broadway, right in front of the old Goldblatt's building at approximately 5:30 a.m. Hennessy pulled up in an older green station wagon and motioned Jamie to get in the car. After dialing a number on his cell phone he handed it to Jamie telling him that Lena would answer the phone. He was to tell her that he was a friend of the Gary Major and to meet him on 2nd Avenue and Broadway at 6:00 a.m. Hennessy then dropped Jamie off at the block of 1st and Broadway and he was instructed to walk to the corner to meet Lena Murdock.

When Murdock showed up Jamie got into the back seat of her car and said that there was someone else in the back seat, she drove off. He said that he did not recognize the man. Mrs. Murdock was then instructed by the unidentified man to drive around the block and when they got back to the light at Broadway, the unidentified man reached over and lassoed some type of cord around her neck and choked her until she didn't move anymore. Jamie said that it took at least one minute before she stopped breathing and moving.

He said that you could hear her gasping for air and that her feet hitting the floor board that's all he could remember.

There was yet another murder that Jamie Jackson unfortunately had to assist in and that was the triple homicide that took place in Glen Park.

On the night of the triple murders of the Crezchek brothers, Jamie Jackson, along with seven other gang members, that were to indulge in this crime activity had to await the orders from the top man out of Chicago. They would have to commit three heinous crimes that took place at the drug house where three Crezchek brothers were getting high at the time.

On the day before this particular crime, the leader of the Cryps held an in-house meeting at an old abandoned building on the west side of town. Attending the meeting was a man that Jamie never seen before. This man was introduced as an extended gang member out of Chicago; they called him Cerni.

He started out as a gang member of the Cryps and ranked the lowest man on the totem pole. He towered himself up to one of the highest ladders in the Chicago mob that a gang member could climb.

Cerni is one of the most clever and slickest men that were to make it big from the slums of Gary, Indiana, into the crime world of Chicago. He was the one who gave the orders for the triple homicide of the Crezchek brothers.

Cerni said that after the Crezchek brothers were taken out, there were to be no more murders until further instructions. Jamie said that was all he heard Cerni talk about, that Cerni and the leader went into another room to finish the conversation.

When Cerni and the King came out of the other room, Cerni proceeded to walk past Jackson, looked at him and nodded, glanced back towards King, put his hand up with a V-sign in front of his nose and walked out the door.

Jackson said that he did not know what the conversation was about that took place between King and Cerni and certainly did not know what the gang sign meant.

Jackson said that the murder of the three Crezchek brothers was well thought-out and very secured by the leaders.

After Cerni left the building, King demanded that there be an in-house meeting without Jackson and told Jackson to go to his "crib" until he was further contacted on what to do. What that was all about Jackson did not know, but he thought it could not be too good, but it later passed and it did not arise again.

JT went to Jacksons crib later on that evening to discuss things with him about what was to take place. JT made a comment to Jackson that King wanted to know why Jackson when assisting the other murders didn't participate in the action. He said that Jamie should be in control of his responsibilities and prove his loyalty to the gang in this next activity or else he would have to be violated.

On the night of the Crezchek brothers' murders, Jackson was to wait for JT and the rest of the gang members to pick him up at the gas station on Georgia Street and 49th Avenue. He was picked up by an older dark blue van with an Illinois license plate.

When he got into the van he said that all the seats and flooring were covered in a durable plastic. He was handed a pair of rubber latex gloves to put on before getting into the van and was also given an artificial mustache to put under his nose, along with a loaded black nine millimeter handgun.

When the van arrived at the drug house, they wasted no time but to get out of the van and immediately they all went into their positions in and out of the house. Jamie had been ordered to be one of the hit men that committed the murders.

Jackson stated that as soon as they got into the house, Mojo told four of the druggies to get out, so they left the drug house premises. Mojo covered the front door and Truce covered the back door, while JT and Jackson were in the living room killing the three Crezchek brothers.

JT pulled out his black nine-milliliter hand gun and told the three brothers to get on the floor, to put their hands behind their back. Erin Crezchek, the oldest brother refused and stepped in front of his two brothers and started arguing with JT. Jackson took out his nine milliliter handgun and back handed Erin in the side of his temple and eye and told him to shut up and to just kneel down on the floor.

JT motioned Jamie to shoot the brother closest to him but he said he froze. JT then took matters into his own hands and began shooting the victims in the back of the head, one by one and then Jackson ran out of the house.

Jackson said that when JT started to shoot the first victim his body immobilized and he instantly knew he had to get out of there and that he had been in the wrong place since day one.

He then left town and went into hiding knowing that if he was ever seen by any of the Cryp gangsters again, that he would be violated without a doubt.

The woman that was with Jamie Jackson had identified herself to Detective Bruder as Nina Colburn. Ms. Colburn declared that she was the woman who had testified in court against him that he had stolen the files from the courthouse. Ms. Colburn stated that she was deathly afraid for her life if she went forward with that information, but that she knew he wasn't guilty of the said crime. She just didn't know what to do.

She then stated to Detective Bruder that she had been in the same room hiding when the three Crezchek brothers were killed.

After Jackson left the house, one of the gang members went inside to check on JT and had spotted her which she then was abducted by him and was taken to a location unknown by blindfold. She was put into a low dim lighted room and was not allowed to take the blindfold off. Ms. Colburn said that she guessed she had been in the room for at least 45 minutes before she heard the door open. She heard the voice of a man to be about the age range of his late 40s to early 50s. He couldn't have been any more blunt with her but to give her an ultimatum as if she wanted to stay alive or not. He continued to explain to her that if she wanted to live then is all she had to do was to cooperate with them and do what she was told to do.

And of course, she had done what anyone else would have done, which was; she was instructed to go to the Gary court house and ask for a woman by the name of Marge. This woman Marge would give her an employment application to fill out. She would then be hired and was then to work until she testified in court against Detective Art Bruder. Then she was to disappear without a trace.

Anyone would have done the same thing if in Ms. Colburn's place, fearing for their life. Nina Colburn has also pointed out that she remembered while at work that when Chief Debroy would speak to her that he chewed cherry mint tobacco, the same tobacco she smelled from the man from when she was abducted. She remembered seeing the name of the flavor of the tobacco on the pouch that Chief Debroy would chew.

The tobacco was found to be an imported product from Italy. In order to get this type of tobacco you had to either be a citizen or correspondent of Italy.

Nina Colburn also stated that there were different people coming and going from Chief Debroy's office. She undoubtedly remembers a young woman about the age of thirty to thirty-two years old who had spoke with a broken accent and looked like she could be from the Italian descendant. This woman had visited Chief Debroy on numerous occasions

Come to find out that this young lady of the Italian descendant seemed to have a lot of business with the chief of police. She was intercepted into the family of the well-known Magistrate Rolando Javez. Back in 1971, Magistrate Javez, was investigated and under surveillance for six months by the FBI. This woman was found to be the daughter of the Magistrate Javez and was born out of wedlock. This woman's name was Natalya Javez who lived in Italy and was smuggling drugs into the United States through tobacco. The cherry mint tobacco had a chemical that absorbed any type of white powdery substance that would protect the smell from leaking out. Ms. Javez was also a member of the secretive circle in Gary, Indiana, and the only way this could have been found out was through a leak from the circle. This young lady was also found to be the half sister of Anthony Crezchek. Her biological last name, Crezchek, was years earlier changed to Javez.

Due to legalities and people her father, Magistrate Rolando Javez knew, threw her criminal case out of court, but the law did charge her with smuggling imported tobacco illegally from a foreign country. She was sentenced to eight years in the United States Federal Prison where she served three years of that.

Nina Colburn told the CIA that she was instructed by one of the Cryp gangsters to make a delivery at Gary National Bank on the corner of Broadway and 5th Avenue. She did not know what it was; but all she could say, is that it was in a sealed yellow envelope and she was to return to Chief Debroy the same little yellow envelope, about one inch by two inches wide, which she said felt like it might contain something metal that weighed about an ounce and perhaps had the shape of a key.

Before leaving the bank, she was instructed by a bank employee to drop the little envelope into a box marked "Evidence" right outside of Chief Debroy's office. She said that as she was driving back to the courthouse, she was curious, so she felt the package and was almost certain that it did feel like some type of a key.

Immediately after the meeting with Nina Colburn, Detective Bruder placed her into the custody of the CIA where she was then established into the witness protection program.

C-13

On the morning of August 9th, 1971, at approximately 8:13 a.m., the CIA took action to have Chief Debroy's office searched. Inside of one of the desk drawers they found a little yellow envelope and inside the envelope was a key. The key had a letter and number marked on it, which was C-13. This key was found to be a safety deposit box key that was the property of the Gary National Bank of Gary, Indiana.

The CIA had given the orders to Detective Bruder to start an investigation at the Gary National Bank. On the afternoon of October the 2nd, Detective Bruder walked into the bank unannounced at 11:59 a.m.

Detective Bruder asked for the supervisor in charge and handed her, Mrs. Jabrowski, a search warrant to search the bank. He ordered Mrs. Jabrowski to give him information about the safety deposit box vault. He had asked her specifically about one safety deposit box, C-13. She was to go and retrieve a key for that box but when she returned she was empty handed. Mrs. Jabrowski told Detective Bruder that she could not locate the key to the box. Mr. Bruder then asked to see the room that the deposit boxes were in and he had also wanted to see the list of names so that he could see which box belonged to whom.

Mrs. Jabrowski left and returned about four to six minutes later to tell Detective Bruder that the vault was not in working conditions, but he could still take a look at the list of names that he wanted to see. She handed him the list of names and he studied the list but could not locate safety deposit box C-13. He then informed her that C-13 was not on the list. She in return explained to him that if C-13 was not on the list was just maybe because there was not such a code for any of the boxes and that maybe they misunderstood the code number. Detective Bruder took Mrs. Jabrowski's explanation to mind and he then left the bank.

On October 4th, 1971, two days later, at just about 6:00 p.m—right in time for the bank to close—Detective Bruder entered the Gary National Bank and went up to the nearest teller. He showed her a search warrant and asked to be directed to Mrs. Jabrowski's office. He entered the room and instructed the teller to turn the computer on. He asked the teller to show him the screen for the safety deposit boxes, then she pulled up the list of names on the computer with no problem.

He began looking the list over and came to C-13, which the name for that deposit box was marked down as belonging to Francis Jackson of Gary, also known as Pastor Francis Jackson—the pastor of the Baptist Church of Gary, Indiana.

Detective Bruder then asked the teller for further information 'about the safety deposit box C-13. The only thing she could come up with is what she found, which was that the Pastor Jackson had rented the box on December the 18th, 1971, one day before the first murder took place.

That following morning Detective Bruder went to pay Pastor Jackson a visit at the Baptist Church in Gary. He approached the pastor about the safety deposit box. The pastor made it clear that he did not know what the detective was talking about, that there had to be some misunderstanding somewhere. The detective left the church and returned the following afternoon to question the pastor once again about the safety deposit box. Again, the pastor denied any knowledge of the box.

About one week later, on October 13th, Detective Bruder went knocking on the church's door one more time. Pastor Francis Jackson let the detective into the church and sat down only to be interrogated by the detective once again. But this time, Pastor Jackson admitted his guilt that he did open the safety deposit box at Gary National Bank.

He pleaded with the detective not to expose him to the public or to anyone in the police department. Detective Bruder gave his word on two conditions: he wanted to know why the pastor was so worried about the police department finding out, and that he wanted to know anything the pastor knew about the safety deposit box. The pastor agreed.

The pastor told to Detective Bruder that he had received a letter in the mail that he was to appear before a judge in the prosecutor's office about a city matter regarding the Baptist Church that needed to be cleared up. When Pastor Jackson walked into the prosecutor's office, the door shut behind him and the only person who appeared was one member of the Cryps. The gang member gave Pastor Jackson no choice but to follow the orders that were given to him. The orders that were given to Pastor Jackson were to go to Gary National Bank and open a safety deposit box in his name. He was to set down the key in the ashtray in the foyer as he walked out the bank door and then leave and go about his business.

Pastor Francis Jackson told Detective Bruder that the gangster had threatened his life. The gangster told him that if he did not do as he was told to do and to keep his mouth shut he would have to endure the consequences.   And this was the reason he did not want anyone from the police department to know of his meeting with Detective Bruder.   He did not want the wrong person to hear the informal scoop that there had been important information leaked out of the circle from the mouth of Pastor Francis Jackson. He stated that he wanted no part of the corruption going on in Gary.

Detective Bruder asked why was it that he, Pastor Jackson was approached by the gangster, why him of all people. Did Anthony Crezchek have anything to do with this and he had replied with the utmost vulnerability that he would do anything for Anthony Crezchek. He tried to assure Detective Bruder that he did not know any other information.

Somehow, Pastor Francis Jackson found himself right in the middle of the secretive circle of the Gary government. There was so much corruption in the making that the citizens of Gary found that they were under the government's black-magic spell just by living in the city.

Pastor Jackson stated that politics had the townspeople in a prison state of mind. The citizens of Gary kept to themselves, and nobody ever talked about anything outside the perimeters of their own personal business.

What has gone drastically wrong with this case that was closed 17 years ago and now has been reopened yet one more time? Who has stirred up this case in high winds and laid the blame on Anthony Crezchek?

Why is it so important that this case be reopened and who are the true guilty parties who really committed these murders? And I do say parties, more than one. It has been proven beyond a reasonable doubt that all these murders could not have been committed by only one person.

Therefore, even if the crimes are being blamed on Anthony Crezchek, the accused in this case, there must have been other parties involved in performing out the acts of the said killings. So in this instance, I would have to ask the court to allow a professional to be brought in to testify that Anthony

Crezchek could not have committed these murders as an individual all by himself.

This brutally hard cold case has for 17 years had been locked in files and been a hush-hush situation because there has not been enough evidence to prove any one person guilty of these said crimes.

To this day, neither the attorney nor prosecutor nor the state's attorney—not even the FBI —could uncover evidence that would put the actual murderers behind bars because of the lack of evidence.

Your Honor, ladies and gentlemen of this court, to this day, there are a multitude of homicide cases that are still open, active cases. And in many of these cases, police believe they know who has committed the crimes, but they don't have enough evidence to put the offender behind bars. Despite all the witnesses who see and hear what the police need to know, the police can only work with what they are told, and too often, people just don't want to get involved.

One of the investigating officers who has

been on the force for over 13 years said it's not just passing observers or spectators who withhold information. He says he is amazed when even the victim's families don't call back. He says, you can leave your card and tell them to call but you never hear anything from anyone.

If the court please, I would like to introduce to you two cases that were put on the back burner, which involve two women who were murdered. Both of these females when the coroner performed an autopsy were identified as being young women both to be about the age of 22-26 years old.

The first case is of a young woman who has yet to be identified. She was found burned at 2nd Avenue and Polk Street on February 26 of this year. This is another sad unsolved case in which with what information the police have for missing persons, this missing person due to the lack of evidence is filed as Jane Doe!

Another unknown victim is a woman whose body was so badly decomposed who was found on Monroe Street. This case was not ruled a homicide, due to lack of evidence!

In the aforementioned cases, the Gary police department believes that these young women had been involved with the secretive circle of the Gary government and had some kind of connection to this case, but due to the lack of evidence, these cases have been ruled and filed as missing persons.

The point being here is that this just goes to show you that with the lack of evidence there is no proof to put anyone behind bars.

Both of these young women were wearing dog tags around their necks. On the back of the dog tags were the engraved words 'CSC,' "Cryps Secretive Circle." Now we can only hypothesize that these two young women were involved somehow with the Cryp gangsters. There were other murdered victims throughout the years that have known to be affiliated with the gang that they too had dog tags around their necks with "Cryps Secretive Circle" engraved on them.

But then we can go deep into how the minds of the Cryps think and work. Did they put the tags on these two girls to cover up something or were the girls truly involved with the gang? That we will never know, only the two deceased girls and the actual killers know the truth.

Year after year, the faces, names and numbers all change, but the end result is still the same; this brings us back to a generation of both black men and women that are currently dying in Gary and the previous years have been the same.

With 103 homicides this year, almost a 65 percent increase over last year, Gary is now, sad to say, in the running once more to lead the nation in per capita homicides cities with a population of 100,000 or more.

And as for every year for decades, the victims are overwhelmingly young, black men and women who were either shot to death or some in disputes over drugs or money and some because of gang affiliation and then there are some for no reason at all.

One of the Chiefs police, chief of Gary, was a police officer for 42 years and he has sat back and watched the outgoing tide of violence in Gary all his life and says that in the 42 years of serving the police department of Gary, Indiana, that 92% of all the crimes that had been committed and are still being committed are never solved due to the lack of evidence!

Unemployment, poverty-stricken, weakened educational system and a very long history of in incompatibility, create a culture susceptible to violent crimes. All the townspeople along with the families and relatives gather where there is a crime, but yet, why the hell not a damn single word is spoken!

Ladies and gentlemen of the jury, who sit in this courtroom today, I ask you, when you go into the deliberation room, to talk amongst you and to take into consideration, that this case that you will be discussing, is just one of thousands of cases that are closed and reopened each year.

There was no evidence found 17 years ago, and it is pertinent that there is no evidence to be found now.

It is extremely obvious that there is corruption that has happened years ago   which continues to exist.

There has been so much corruption that this case has been reopened without any striking piece of evidence. There are too many pieces of evidence that have not as of yet been recovered to this day.

As you certainly can see, just like other cases that this case, like so many others, lies in the graves of the dead. Your Honor, due to the lack of evidence, I ask that this case be laid to rest!

Anyone can obviously see that this case has without a doubt been corrupted since the beginning. How long will the courts allow the prosecution side to continue to make a practical joke out of the judicial system?

The prosecution side has attempted to make a case without a single piece of evidence. There has been no evidence found or recovered to this day. What other court system would allow such a mess to continue to burden the lives of other people to no avail? No one would even consider to let a court case to be brought into the courtroom without any circumstantial evidence. Without any evidence for proof of any crime being committed, how and why would anyone be allowed to bring into the court a play of charades?

As we go into the life testimony of Anthony Crezchek you will hear from the child that came from deep within the soul and mind of the little boy who was so hideously abused for most of his life. You will be able to hear the chillness surrounded by his voice. The cruelty that led him astray. The bitterness that spit from his lips into hatred. The little boy who has lost his life but who still has his sanity for some inexplicable reason.

You will hear from Mr. Crezchek himself how life has truly been nothing but pure hell! His life was a pure nightmare with torture, misery agony and a torment.

I will ask only one thing of you, ladies and gentlemen, who sit in the jury box and that is to please, put this case to rest and let Mr. Crezchek as his life was once left as a little boy into the man he is to this day, let him keep what sanity he has left. Due to this shocking and disgraceful case, he has been slapped in the face recurrently time and time again.

Each time the out come of this scatological and overbearing blame that is placed on Anthony Crezchek, it is that much more that the dignity of these proceedings is compromised. It is not only that Crezchek's humane rights are being degraded but the judicial system is being played and disrespected. Indiana's judicial systems reputation is being ruined by scandalmongers who pretend to be law abiding citizens. But in reality all they are doing is using the system to cover up their unlawful acts.

Now you can sit back and listen to how life has blackened Mr. Crezchek's childhood and decide for yourselves if he should be able to keep what sanity he has left or will you allow this innocent man to be tortured every time the city of Gary, Indiana, chooses to hide its corruption by reopening the Crezchek files to shift the blame off of itself. Listen carefully with only your ears to what you're about to hear ...

The Crezchek Files

The Life Testimony

Of

Anthony Crezchek

Due to the fact that Anthony Crezchek has had enough tumult and disorder in his life the court has come to a decision that Mr. Crezchek will not be allowed to take the witness stand, but that I as his attorney, will present to you, ladies and gentlemen of this court, Anthony Crezchek's sworn life testimony!

For as long as Anthony Crezchek could remember, this is how his life testimony of his childhood growing up took place. The statement you are about to hear are all acts leading up that would be convincing that a person or persons could commit all seven murders such as these of the Crezchek family.

Now, ladies and gentlemen of the jury, I am not going to tell you in *my* words the life testimony of Anthony Crezchek, but in *his* own words that came from *his* mouth. I will read from this manuscript that I have here in my hands the recorded written life testimony of Anthony Crezchek.

I must warn each and every one of you who sit in this courtroom today that this sworn statement that I am about to read to all of you contains graphic details that some of you may not want to hear.

If there is anyone here that does not wish to sit in this courtroom during the reading of this sworn statement of Anthony Crezchek's life testimony, you should leave now, before the reading begins. If you do not leave this court room now, after I begin the reading of this statement, you will not be allowed to get up and leave.

So, please, feel free to get up and leave this courtroom now!

(Pause)

MR. BRUMENTHAL: Your Honor, may I begin?

JUDGE CHEDISTER: Yes, Mr. Brumenthal, you may start the reading of the testimony.

MR. BRUMENTHAL: Your Honor, ladies and gentlemen of the jury, I will now begin the reading of the sworn statement of Anthony Crezchek's life testimony.

MR. BRUMENTHAL: Will you please state your name for the record?

ANTHONY CREZCHEK: Anthony Crezchek.

MR. BRUMENTHAL: Mr. Crezchek, do you understand what you are doing here today?

ANTHONY CREZCHEK: Yes.

MR. BRUMENTHAL: Do you understand that you are about to give a sworn statement here today?

ANTHONY CREZCHEK: Yes.

MR. BRUMENTHAL: You do understand that the court has decided against you taking the witness stand? You do understand this, right?

ANTHONY CREZCHEK: Yes.

MR. BRUMENTHAL: And you do understand that

once you start this sworn statement, even if you should decide to stop, that whatever you have sworn to will be permissible in court for open reading? You do understand this, don't you?

ANTHONY CREZCHEK: Yes.

MR. BRUMENTHAL: Thank you. Now, Mr. Crezchek, I just want you to relax. The court reporter will be typing your statement on her stenograph machine. That's the machine that you see right there in front of her, okay?

ANTHONY CREZCHEK: Okay.

MR. BRUMENTHAL: I want you to take your time and start from the beginning. Go as far back into your childhood as you can, and just tell me in your own words what you remember, okay? That's easy enough, isn't it?

ANTHONY CREZCHEK: Yeah. I guess so.

(Pause)

MR. BRUMENTHAL: Okay, Mr. Crezchek, you can begin anytime you're ready.

(Pause)

ANTHONY CREZCHEK: Umm … I don't know where to start.

MR. BRUMENTHAL: Why don't you begin-well, let's do it this way. Start by telling me at what age do you remember yourself as a child.

ANTHONY CREZCHEK: Okay.

(Pause)

MR. BRUMENTHAL: Okay, so how young do you remember yourself as a child? Do you remember yourself at the age of two, three, five? What age can you remember yourself as a child?

ANTHONY CREZCHEK: Umm ... I think I was probably, maybe, around like two, three years old.

MR. BRUMENTHAL: Okay. That's a good start. Now, just tell me what you remember about being that age. Do you remember good things, bad things or happy and sad things, what are you thinking about right now?

ANTHONY CREZCHEK: Well, I guess when I was like two years old, no, wait… I don't know how old I was, but I just remember not being too happy as a kid. I never got to play with any friends.

Is a matter of fact, I don't think that I ever had any friends. I don't remember having any friends. No, now that I really think about it, I didn't have any friends!

I had to always stay at home with my parents and take

care of them.

It's funny because when I think of the age three, I can easily remember bad things. Not a single good thing can I remember. At the age of three, I was still in diapers or I was supposed to be. My mother and father didn't buy diapers for me. I mean they didn't change me too many times the way they were supposed to. I would be in the same diaper for hours, days at a time. I would get diaper rash so bad that I still have light blotches on my skin down there. Yeah, the rash burned my skin so bad that it left my skin scarred and discolored. Really it just looks like it's a different color than some of my other skin.

Sometimes my mother would let me run around the house without a diaper on. Maybe I should just say that I had to run around without a diaper on. I think she was too lazy to change me or something. I know I can remember that sometimes when I got a diaper rash really bad that my mom and dad would hit me on my bare butt. It would hurt something awful. It kept on stinging and the hurt wouldn't go away. Like a bee sting that wouldn't stop after it stung you.

It just kept on stinging you!

I think that I didn't know it at the time, but I believe that they would spank me for going to the bathroom on the floor. But you know, what could I have done when I didn't have a diaper on. It wasn't my fault ya know. But I guess they both thought it was my fault. Everything was my fault! How can they have blamed shit on me when I probably didn't even understand any of it? I was too young to know any better. At least that's what I think, I guess.

I was only three years old, so what did I know. Yeah, they would spank me on my butt. They took a belt to me. They were nothing but drug-addicted mother fuckers! To think of the shit they did to me. The shit they let other people do to me.

I don't understand why somebody didn't help me …

I think one day, I had shit in my diaper, and it was burning my butt, so I took it off and was playing in it. I remember my mother pushing me down on the floor, and I remember rolling and rolling, it seemed as though I would never stop. That's the first time I got my arm broken. That fucking bitch pushed me down the basement stairs and I rolled down each dam stair until I hit the bottom and landed on my arm.

Ever since then, I have this protruding bone that looks and it feels like it's coming out of my elbow. Look, see, right here. You can see it right here. See? It used to hurt something terrible, but I guess I just got used to it after a while, and it became what belonged to me like other things did.

When I use to sit down and eat cereal my father use to take the bowl of cereal and pour it over my head. They use to sit there and laugh at me. At first when they started doing things like that to me, I laughed with them, but as I got older and realized it really wasn't funny is when the other abuse started. Although, in reality, the abuse had already started but I was so young maybe I just didn't understand what was going on.

You know, I had always promised myself that I would not ever do to my kids as I have been done from my parents.

And the shit they done to me, they were FUCKERS. REALLY MOTHER FUCKERS!

I still forgive them to this day. I think. I don't know.

My mother, she would always tell me how she loved me and then Bam! I knew something was going to happen.

I used to sit in the corner of the living room and watch both my parents shoot up their drugs right into their arm. When they couldn't stick a needle in their arm anymore they stuck the needle where ever they could, where ever their body would allow the needle to stick.

Sometimes, I was afraid that they were going to stick me with a needle. I don't know why, but I got that leery feeling.

When they didn't have their fix, as I call it, they were just as even more unpleasant as they were being high.

At times, when they got high, they would just sit there, dad on the couch and mom on the chair and stare for hours as if they were the living dead. The house could have burned down and they wouldn't have felt a thing. And then there would be other times when they were so high that they would get so violent, but just with me, not anyone else.

I really just hated when my mom would run out of cigarettes. I knew then I would have to go to the store and steal again, for her. I knew what could happen when she got her cigarettes!

She would make me open the pack up and then light one for her, and if I didn't she would try to shove it down my throat. One time she pushed me up against the wall, and with her knee clamping me so I couldn't get away, she shoved the cigarette in my mouth and some of it went down my throat and I would end up swallowing it. And sometimes I would even cough up blood and throw up.

Then when her cigarette was lit, the inevitable would happen.

Then my mom would roll up my sleeves of my shirt and take a lit cigarette and burn my arms. She would cram the cigarette so hard into my skin that the cigarette would go out.

I remember one time she made me take my pants off. She was so dam cruel and so dam cold. The BITCH burned the inside of my thighs. I thought she was going to burn my penis. When she would burn me down there, it hurt so bad I couldn't sleep for days.

Yeah, it hurt so bad. She didn't even care if she hurt me, that bitch. FUCKING CUNT!

My mother told me that she had to burn me with the cigarettes, that if I got lost, they would be able to find me through the burn marks, that all the kids got branded. I have scars all over my black ass body from her burning me. I got sick sometimes when she burned me real bad. One time I got so feverish and needed doctor care but she wouldn't let me go.

After she would do things like that to me, she wouldn't let me go to school. I missed so much school that I would get expelled and even got kicked out of some schools. A counselor one time had called me out of class and had asked me if everything was all right at home and why was it that I was missing so many days of school. I didn't want my parents to get in trouble, so I lied to the counselor and said that I just didn't want to be in school. I didn't want to be there. She had no choice but to take my word for it. What else could she do?

There was one time when my mom was as high as a kite on heroin and one minute she was all lovey dovey to me; the next minute, she was like a bomb that exploded. She grabbed me and started to push me down the hallway into the kitchen, then pushed me down the stairs into the basement and locked the door so I couldn't get out.

But little did she know that after a while that I got smart and had hidden food down there. She would lock me down in the basement, for maybe, like, maybe two days at a time.

One time when she pushed me down the stairs, I think I broke my arm. I think it was broken because it hurt really bad and it looked like a bone was sort of sticking-I mean, I think it was sort of popping out of my skin. I had to make a sling for it myself, because she wouldn't let me go to the doctor.

In a way, I was relieved to be in that basement, then I knew she wouldn't bother me for a while. I was safe!

My dad, he would just go with whatever she said or did. I think he was more dead than alive anyway. I don't think he functioned hardly at all. But he had his days of coming alive when it came to me. One day, I told him to please stop the drugs, but he took a hold of me and started shaking me like I was a jug of Kool-Aid or something. My neck got hurt; I think even I had whiplash from him shaking me so hard. My neck was so stiff, I couldn't turn it one way or the other.

One night, my father made me go to my bedroom, which I really dreaded, because I knew what was about to happen to me. It was probably about twenty minutes later that he came in my room with a belt in his hands.

I can still to this day recall the way that belt looked. The buckle was made out of cast iron that was made for him by my grandfather. It had a shape of a bell and when he hit me it almost knocked the wind right out of me because of the buckle weighing so much.

My father would grab hold of my one hand and then start swinging that dam belt at me and he would hit me anywhere he could.

He told me if I cried, I would get it even more, so I tried not to let him hear me cry out loud so he would stop. He said, 'big boys don't cry!'

God, it hurt so badly! My little body had welts all over and lots of times I even started bleeding. I can almost feel the numbness all over again, just as if it were right here with me.

That was another time that I should have gone to the hospital, but my father would not take me. Instead, he gave me Band-Aids to put on. In fact, he just threw the dam things at me and told me to put them on myself.

I was so use to them hitting me and yelling at me and doing to me what ever it was they wanted to do to me. I guess it was sort of normal to me in my life with them. But I knew it hurt. It hurt so bad! Not just the physical abuse, but the mental abuse too.

They use to tell me that I was nothing but a little bastard! That I was no good and would never be nothing. They would laugh at me and tell me how ugly I was, that I shouldn't be allowed to go outside at all so no one could see me. They said that if anyone seen me that they would do nothing but laugh at me and that's why no kids would ever play with me, that's why I didn't have any friends.

Yeah, that's what they would tell me. You know, they thought I was stupid or something. I know why I didn't have any friends, and it was because of them not letting me have any.

One day, they were laughing at me about that and I got mad and told them that it was because of them that I didn't have any friends. I guess I should have never said that because my father took his glass pipe he was using for drugs and smashed it right into my face.

The glass broke when he hit me with it and some of the glass imbedded in my skin on my face. I had to go in the bathroom and lock the door and pick out the little pieces of glass out of my face.

My face has scars on it because of it! You can see the scares right here. See, right here.

"THAT ROTTEN SON-OF-A-BITCH!" Yeah, that's what he was.

Sometimes I had to stay in my bedroom for a couple of days at a time without coming out. My parents wouldn't even let me out to go to the bathroom. I would have to keep on the same pants that I went bathroom in on or else they would beat the shit out of me.

And sometimes they let me out and checked to see if I had the remains after going bathroom on myself, if it were-was still in my pants, but, it didn't matter, because I never knew what mood they were both in.

Yeah, depending how they felt and what kind of mood they were in at the time, my mom would take a pair of scissors and cut the pants off of me and rub the pants in my face.

She was so mean. So cruel!

She would rub the pants so hard in my face that the shit would go in my mouth and up my nose, it even got into my eyes. After she done that, they would make me stand up with my arms by my side and make me smile.

Yeah, they made me smile so my mouth would open and shit would actually fall out onto my lips. They would sit there and laugh at me. I wanted to throw up so bad!

But if I threw up, they made me lick it up off the floor. And if I didn't do it, they would start pulling my hair so hard that they yanked patches out of my head. That's why my hair is thinned in some places, and that's why I just shave my head bald.

One time when I was down on the floor licking throw up off of the floor, I just remember being kicked in the side of the face. I can remember falling down on the floor and my father yelling at me to get up or I would have to go down to the basement.

Most of the time, I didn't care because I sort of wanted to go to the basement, that's where I'd be safe from hell! That was my heaven! Yeah, my heaven. So I would just lay there on the floor.

I don't know why they did what they did but, is all I know is that they really didn't mean to hurt me. They just did what they did because of the drugs.

I understand a lot better now that I am older.

When I was a little kid, I was so adapted to the lifestyle my parents had given me that I guess I really didn't know any better. My body was so routinely battered that I thought that was normal, because I didn't know anything else.

Of all the things, I mean, all of the abuse my mother and father had done unto me, I just couldn't understand one thing, and that was the sexual abuse. How could they let people, especially my relatives, abuse me sexually! They're all fucking sick! It's just fucking nuts!

(Big sigh)

"My God!"

I had this one auntie, Auntie Lena, I thought she was the one that I would have been able to trust, but I was wrong.

My parents bought some drugs through her I guess, because for some reason, the Cryps had stopped selling to them. Well when I was about eight years old, she came to our house to collect the money from my mother and father, but they of course didn't have it.

She looked at me standing in the corner, which I felt weird from that strange look she gave me and told my parents that she would take it up with me down in the basement. They just turned as if they couldn't see me standing there, and my auntie took a hold of my hand and took me to the basement, where she then molested me.

Every time my auntie came over to our house, I knew what was going to happen. It felt so odd when she would touch me all over my body, but it just became a repetitive act between us that my little mind became ill in thoughts. Who in there right mind would do this shit to their nephew, to a kid? Who?

I prayed to God to make them stop!

I was only eight years old, for Christ's sake!

See my fingertips on both my hands? Well that happened when it was real cold outside. It was a hard cold winter one year and my mother told me to get out of the house. She barely let me grab my coat when she was pushing me out the door.

I didn't think she or my father could stoop any lower than what they already have with me but I guess I was wrong again.

In the morning of that actual day, my mother was going through the refrigerator and realized that there was nothing in there to eat.

My mother was so mean to me. I guess being the young age as I was, it trained my mind to be deathly afraid of her.

The way she would yell and scream at me. When she raised her hand up in the air at me, my whole body would twinge up so tight.

She took the belt to me one time when I accidentally spilled my cup of water on the floor. Her eyes looked like they were going to pop out. She pushed me down on the floor and grabbed me by the leg and dragged me to my bedroom.

She made me lay across my bed so my arms and legs-legs-yeah my legs would dangle off the sides of the bed then she would start hitting me with that dam belt.

Then she would start hitting me, like I said, with that dam belt, and if I cried she would only hit me that much harder. She would start crying and say that Jesus had to suffer for us and now we have to suffer for him.

I was sitting down at the kitchen table and I could hear my father stomping down the hall. I kept my head tilted down towards the table and he just came over to me and grabbed onto the back of the chair and started forcing it back and forth and rocking it until I fell on the floor.

He yelled at me to get up so I did. He began to slap me in the face. He would slap my face from one side to the other. I kept backing up, and when I knew I got close to the kitchen sink I knew I could get down fast and climb into the cabinet under the sink.

He would keep kicking the door, till it broke one day, then his foot would go through the broken door and sometimes it would hit me. I stayed there all squeezed up until I knew for sure he was gone.

There would be a lot of times when they would be after me and I would hide in the kitchen cabinets, they never looked in there. I don't know why. I made a wall out of a old sheet that I found in the garbage outside. So if they did look in the cabinets I couldn't be found by them. I would sleep in there sometimes too.

At Christmas time, some of my aunts and uncles would come over to our house to spend the day with us. But the only aunts and uncles that ever came over were the ones that like to get high.

So what does that tell you?

Well, on one Christmas year I can remember them coming over and when it was time to open presents, my parents, aunts and uncles, they all exchanged gifts, and then my mother would throw one to me.

It wasn't even wrapped.

It was a jelly jar with mold starting to grow because she didn't even wash the jar out.

Then my father told me that if I cleaned it out that I could use it for a beer mug. Then my parents practically threw me out of the living room. I went into my bedroom and got into the closet. I peeked through the hole and sat there for a while watching all of them tie rubber tubing around each one of their arms. Sticking a needle in and watch them fall-out. That's how I would spend most of my Christmases. Christmases never ever seemed like a holiday to me. Just another day in hell, that's all!

This one particular Christmas when I got that dam jelly jar, I went outside and stood on the back steps, and I heard the neighbor kids two houses away playing in their yard with their new sleds and wearing their new boots and coats. I don't know what came over me, but I got real mad, and the more I thought about it the more angry I got. So I went back into the house and grabbed that dam jar and went back outside.

It was like I just started going crazy and really don't know what came over me, like I said. I took the jar and threw it as hard as I could on the back walk. It broke into a thousand pieces and it made me feel good to do it too. I sat down on the ground in the cold snow and cried my eyes out.

As I looked down at the ground I thought I heard someone talking to me and when I looked up there stood Pastor Jackson. I can still see him reaching down with his arms to pick me up off that dam cold ground.

He held me so tight that I never felt so close to anyone like that before. Never! Not even my own parents. Yeah, not even my lousy parents.

I could feel him tremble, tears rolled down his face, and then he put me down and led me to his car. I—or I mean both of us—got in his car. He handed me a present. It was a Christmas present. It was the best present I ever got. Truly, it was the best present I ever got.

It was a Bible.

To this day, I still read it. It's leather and has the red wording, big words. It even has tabs on the pages. When he first gave it to me, when I opened it up, inside the bible about right in the middle of the book was a bookmark.

On one side there was a picture of Jesus, and the other side said, "I and the Lord are always in your life. The Lord and I will always love you. Amen, my son!"

I treasure that Bible. I knew then that I had something to look forward to the next Christmas.

Ya know, some people can't understand why I could never stand still. The reason for that is 'cause my father, one day, made me go in the kitchen and stand in the middle of the floor. That floor was so ugly. It was squares. He made me stand in one square with both my feet. I had to hold my arms out like a bird. My arms would hurt so bad. When he went into the other room to get his fix, I would rest them down by my side for a fast second. I could hear him coming down the hall, 'cause he dragged his feet. I had enough time to raise my arms back up in the air before he got there.

Sometimes he would do his drugs in the kitchen so he could watch me. He made sure I wouldn't move from that square. And if I put my arms down where he could notice he would make me stand on one foot. He use to sit there and laugh at me and told me I looked like a pelican. Well if I would put my arms down he would take a piece of rope and wrap it around my ankle and then yank on it so I would fall down. I would fall on my back most of the time. I think maybe that's why I have problems with my back so much.

And if I cried when I fell, he would make me get right back up, and he would do it again.

One time, I refused to get back into the square, so he tied the rope around both my legs and dragged me from one end of the house to the other end. He laughed at me cause I tried to grab the rope and was not fast enough. He yanked at it even harder that time and he would pull it so fast and hard that my head would hit the floor.

One time when he was dragging me, my head got caught on a nail that was sticking out of the floor. I think it was a nail. I didn't feel it though until he stopped. Then the pain flared up like a ball of fire. I touched the back of my head and could feel and see the blood on my hand. I told my father and even tried to show him the blood on my hand, but I guess he didn't care. He told me to just go to the bathroom and put toilet paper on it. That I would be okay. Not to be a baby about it. He did stop it though but only for that time being.

Over on the table sat old cans of opened corn that still had the top of it halfway on and off. The top had rusty rigid edges like a old knife. I went over and picked the rusty lid up and stood there and held it tight. I closed my eyes and pictured that I walked right up to my father without any fear. Just as I was about to slash his throat I was awakened from my trans of thought by my father. He asked me what the hell I thought I was going to do with that lid. I tried to deny what was the truth and would not give in either. Good thing too, 'cause he was getting ready to slap the shit out of me. What a fucking idiot! Mother fucker! Yeah, he could be a big jerk sometimes.

Too bad my actions weren't fast enough to do the trick. It would have been over long time ago. I wouldn't have had to suffer the way I did. Maybe! Who knows ...

Speaking of the rope, there was a game they'd like

to play with me. They, meaning my uncles. When they use to come over to get high with my parents, they made me run from them, and they would try to lasso me like I was a animal or something. Sometimes they would get me, and sometimes they would try for hours without roping me a single time. I would get rug burns the times they did get me. My uncles would pull my pants down and tell me to take down my underwear. They said that made it easier for them to rope me.

I knew what was going to happen when they came over to play that game. They would end up, one by one, taking me into the bedroom. I should have castrated the bastards!

They would make me touch them while they touched me back. It made me so ashamed of everything and fearful that I couldn't trust anyone. The one uncle would make me do oral sex on him. He would hold my head and force his you-know-what almost down my throat. One time I thought to myself that he wasn't going to get away with it. So when he did it the next time, I bit down on him, but he slugged the side of my face as hard as he could.

Then he flipped me over and finished on my backside. I should have cut the son of a bitch's dick off!

Well, I guess I was just use to it. The abuse I mean. But you never get used to somebody trying to violate your mind though. That's one thing nobody could ever take away from me. My thoughts. No one could tell me what to think or could ever know what I was thinking about. That's what kept my sanity. Probably the only thing that kept my sanity.

Lot of times, I felt like digging my own grave. I just wanted to dig a hole and crawl inside and bury myself. I thought about running away a bunch of times, but one time my father beat the shit out of me when I tried. Yeah, he beat me with a cord the one time I did try. The cord was intentionally shredded with a knife so that when they beat me with it the wires that were exposed would cut my skin. So I thought it be better if I didn't try no more. But if I knew I could of got away with it, I would have run away and never went back …

I could have taken care of myself, ya know. After

all, I really took care of myself anyway. My mom never cooked for me or washed my clothes or anything. There wasn't any food in the house anyway for her to cook. The only thing I really got to eat was lunch meat. If we had it. If I got really hungry, I had to steal food. I didn't like to steal, so sometimes I would go behind stores and restaurants and get inside the big garbage cans and get the food out of there.

Like I said, It wasn't all that bad. They threw away some good food sometimes. Well, I guess if you can look past it being in the garbage can then it really is good food. I liked when they would throw out cakes and pies. That was the best part of picking garbage there. Every bite I took, I ate it very slowly so that I could remember how good it tasted. I never knew if I would get the chance to eat another piece of pie.

That ended after a while cause someone had told my mother that I was going through the garbage and she told me if I was hungry to go to work. She said that I was stealing that food. That it wasn't mine to take.

That night when she found it out that I was taking

the food out from the garbage, she made me stand in the corner of the kitchen with tape on my mouth. It was that grey tape. It was thick tape. It was really sticky. I couldn't take the tape off until she did. I wasn't supposed to take it off. She told me that if I stole any more food that she would pull off the tape again. And she would rip the tape as fast as she could off my mouth. That hurt so bad. My lips, some of the skin came off. My lips felt like they were burned. I couldn't sleep for, like, two days. The burning feeling wouldn't go away.

And when my lips got dry from not drinking anything, it felt like all my mouth was falling off my face. I could hardly touch anything with them, and if I did, my eyes would get teared up. I would even cry sometimes because it hurt. I could hardly take the pain. I would go in my bedroom so the wind would not blow on my lips. I use to lie down on my bed and meditate for the release of the pain I was feeling. My lips were so raw and tender they would throb for hours. Then they went numb.

I tried to be good. I didn't think I was being bad. I don't know. Maybe if I was a better kid, my parents would not have done to me what they did. I don't know. I don't think it's my fault. There I go again.

The therapist I use to go to said I needed to stop blaming myself for the abuse I was taking. He said I had no reason to even think that I was a bad kid, because I wasn't a bad kid. That it was all my parents and their damn drugs. The drugs took over both their minds. He said that that's what drugs do to you. Drugs eat your brain cells up and make you a dysfunctional person. They must have been pretty dysfunctional then to do what they did to me. People say I'm messed up, but why do you figure? Hell yes, I must be messed up. I mean, what the fuck? If they got what I did, they'd be messed up too.

My parents were pretty messed up too I guess. I use to hear some people talking about that crap. I don't know. I don't know anything anymore, I guess.

At first when my parents would do drugs, I would have to sit there and watch them. Is all I could do was to just sit there and cringe. I wanted to let the couch swallow me up in its pillows. I would have to sit there and see them fill up the syringe and then stick the needle in their arms. They would fall out almost as fast as they could put the syringe down.

One day, an attorney came to our house. I was sitting at the kitchen table eating a piece of bologna. There was a knock at the door, and my dad yelled at me to go get it. The man stepped inside the house, and then my father told me to leave the room. I went into my bedroom, went into my closet, where there was a little hole in the wall, and I could see and hear pretty much everything that was going on in the living room.

The man took out some papers out of his briefcase and handed them to my father. My father asked him what the hell the papers were for, and the man told him that they were adoption papers. I guess Pastor Jackson wanted to adopt me and my parents weren't having it. I don't know why; they weren't doing anything for me anyway. I have to say that I was a bit surprised when I heard that the papers were from Pastor Jackson. That was the first time I heard of it.

My father threw the papers back at the man

and told him to shove the papers up his ass! The attorney told my father that they were better off to let the pastor adopt me rather than having to appear in court, and he said that it was better to settle out of court, because otherwise the whole truth would have to come out then. By that time, my mother had come into the living room and said that Jackson will never get the right to me. Then she had asked him to leave the house.

You know, when I was a kid, at that time, I could never understand what she meant by saying that Jackson would never get a right to me. But now that I am older I think that over the years of getting to know the pastor, things have come together and make sense now.

If nobody can figure it out, then I'm not about to explain it to them either.

So don't ask!

As I got older, into my teen years, the abuse began to slow down. All the hitting, punching, banging my head against the walls, the burning cigarettes, all the physical and sexual abuse that throbbed my mind and body finally started coming to a holt. My parents were so strung out by that time they had no strength left in their weak bodies.

The last time they tried to hurt me I can remember clear as daylight. I had just about all I could have taken over the years, and I decided that I could out power the both of them, so I did! I knew in my mind that I could finally win this battle that had taken me over for years as a child.

I WON! I WAS FREE!

So you see, all I know is pain all my life—physical pain, verbal pain and emotional pain!

I often wonder if they ever did love me. They had to; I know they did. It was just the drugs that gave them their loss of consciousness when it came to me. They just didn't know what they were doing. I don't ever remember my parents being sober. No, they were never clean from drugs that I know of. I always pictured them being high as kites, flying side by side.

You know, I just wanted them to cuddle me and love me without hurting me, but, I never got that kind of love.

You would think that it shouldn't hurt to be a child, but sometimes it does, and it hurts really bad. Being a battered child means hoping your parents will be in a good mood, but knowing you couldn't trust them even if they were.

You know they say that there are some abusers who will never change and removing them from society is the only way of dealing with them.

Need I say any more?

Think I'm done!

Closing to the Court

This case has been closed and reopened by the prosecution side multiple times and for what reasons are still questionable. They have brought this case to the courtroom with intent to go to trial.

I ask the court: only one question; Not only based on inclusion of evidence, but there is no evidence at all brought into this court room. Without any evidence to prove my client was guilty of these heinous crimes, why was this case, or let me rephrase that please, how could this case have even made it this far into the judicial system without a single piece of evidenc*e?*

Is the Gary government the only corrupted party in this case or does this just keep going further into different political jurisdictions?

Ladies and gentlemen of this court, we can only speculate as to what really happened to the members of the Crezchek family.

Throughout these proceedings, you have heard accusations by people who were found to be incapable of telling the truth. You have seen a court room of socialists who have righteously down poured nothing but criticism where it didn't belong. You have seen poor judgment after poor judgment sitting on the witness stand with nothing but corrupted words erupting from their guilty mouths.

There has not been a single attorney in this courtroom who has presented one piece of evidence to support the accusations brought against my client.

On the date of May 1st, 1974, a specially appointed judge ruled that the state of Indiana could not seek a penalty sentence against Anthony Crezchek, who previously had two sentences overturned due to "fundamental principles of fairness."

For the past 17 years there has been charges brought up against Anthony Crezchek for the murders of his parents and extended family. Crezchek did not receive a fair trial and has always maintained his noninvolvement in the crime.

The state had withheld favorable evidence which resulted of a gunshot residue test termed "inconclusive" as to whether Anthony Crezchek had fired the gun that killed the three Crezchek brothers.

The court also found that the counsel's assistant in the 1974 trial provided ineffective assistance. In fact, he was found to have been working for the prosecution side. He was so intimidated by the police state atmosphere surrounding the trial that he didn't sit at the same table as Crezchek. He also failed to interview prosecution witnesses.

Before the trial was dismissed, the

prosecution tried to claim there had been an honest mistake. Maybe a misunderstanding and even lost papers.

Everyone knows it's a lie.

Indeed, there has been a felony committed here, and someone needs to go to jail.

In 1979, the prosecution tried to re-sentence his over ride. The Indiana Supreme Court vacated Crezchek's second trial, finding that black people had been systematically excluded from the pool from which the jury had been chosen.

In fact, half of the black population had been eliminated from the jury pool for the previous 15 years.

All these Lake County Superior Court judges have been forced to rescue themselves from Crezchek's case. Two were disqualified for blatant conflicts of interest, and the other left the bench to enter an alcohol rehabilitation center.

Lake County judges, they say, have become as soft as Marion County judges, who are notoriously easy on criminals.

But whose side do they favor?

Besides, the liberal judge needs to be accountable for neglecting their duty to put criminals away and to keep our community safe. These judges have given the wrong criminal the difficult hardship. All the criminals and predators in this case should serve their time.

In my closing to the court, I am going to read to you a signed and dated deposition that was taken on the date of May 7th, 1974.

Now this witness testified under oath that the Crezchek files was nothing but a big plot to cover some of the political assets of the estranged government as we are learning to know it. The individual known as "Witness Jack" can be considered the most crucial witness in this case.

Witness Jack was put into a witness protection program before going under oath.

Witness Jack testified that the following have been known to take part in legendary acts of unkindness: William Swartz, from the city of Gary, Indiana website. Mitch Lawrence, from West Side

Photography, and three unidentified white men from Miller Beach Days.

All five have been involved with the one witness who could turn things around in this case. All the rubbish mixed together with hate and spite could have been finally dismissed. But most of the city's people carry fear deep within and tend to keep dark secrets far well beneath the grounds dirt!

Why has the witness denied any wrong doings of the above mentioned? This witness is the only crucial person who would be able to tell the court exactly action for action which led to the mishap and misfortune of the Crezchek family.

Before this particular witness took the stand, there was another witness that could not meet the criteria of the court. This person since they were under the age of eighteen was kept under strict supervision of the United States National Guard for their own protection.

They were allowed, however, to give a statement under oath to the United States Supreme Court in the State of Illinois. The gender of this person is not known, due to the children's privacy act of the Humane Civil Rights Act, which children are 100 percent protected from any lawful abiding harm ensuring the privacy and safety of minors.

Ladies and gentlemen, due to the age of this particular witness, only certain segments of this testimony will be read in this courtroom. It goes as follows:

STATE'S ATTORNEY: How do you know the witness?

UNDERCOVER WITNESS: I can't tell you.

STATE'S ATTORNEY: Do you live close to the witness?

UNDERCOVER WITNESS: I can't tell you that.

STATE'S ATTORNEY: Are you related to the

witness?

UNDERCOVER WITNESS: I can't tell you that.

STATE'S ATTORNEY: Are you about the same age as the witness?

UNDERCOVER WITNESS: I can't tell you that.

STATE'S ATTORNEY: Okay then. In your own words, please tell us everything that you know about this witness.

UNDERCOVER WITNESS: Okay. The woman is a very nice person, but she is extremely dangerous! She has been involved with all five men.

STATE'S ATTORNEY: What five men are you talking about? And when you say she was involved, how was she involved with these men?

UNDERCOVER WITNESS: William Swartz, Mitch Lawrence, and the three unidentified white men from Miller Beach Days. She had marital affairs with all five men since she was 17 years old. Some people say she was a kept woman.

STATE'S ATTORNEY: What do you mean by "kept woman?"

UNDERCOVER WITNESS: You know, she had sex with them in return for them taking care of her.

STATE'S ATTORNEY: Taking care of her? Please explain this.

UNDERCOVER WITNESS: Well, she has sex with these men, and in return for her sexual behavior they pay for her house, clothes and whatever else it may be that she wants.

STATE'S ATTORNEY: So, in other words, they give her money for having sex with them, right?

UNDERCOVER WITNESS: Right.

STATE'S ATTORNEY: All of these five men pay her expenses?

UNDERCOVER WITNESS: Yes, they do.

STATE'S ATTORNEY: Do these men actually go and pay her bills for her themselves?

UNDERCOVER WITNESS: No. They could never risk getting caught.

STATE'S ATTORNEY: Who would they have to worry about catching them?

UNDERCOVER WITNESS: Well, first of all; their wives, second, they are all in politics, so they had to hide everything they had done.

STATE'S ATTORNEY: I understand that this woman became very wealthy.

UNDERCOVER WITNESS: Yes, she did, or, I should say, she still is very wealthy. She had the easy life all along.

STATE'S ATTORNEY: You mentioned earlier that she was a dangerous woman. What makes you think that?

UNDERCOVER WITNESS: Anybody will tell you that if you get on her bad side who knows what could happen to you.

STATES ATTORNEY: Have you seen her do things to other people?

UNDERCOVER WITNESS: No, but I heard things.

STATE'S ATTORNEY: Things? What kind of things have you heard?

UNDERCOVER WITNESS: That she can be really mean.

STATE'S ATTORNEY: What things have you heard that she has done to people?

UNDERCOVER WITNESS: I can't tell you.

STATE'S ATTORNEY: What can you tell me?

UNDERCOVER WITNESS: I don't know.

STATE'S ATTORNEY: Can you tell me anything about this woman?

UNDERCOVER WITNESS: I was told I can't say anything.

STATE'S ATTORNEY: Who told you that you

could not say anything about this woman?

UNDERCOVER WITNESS: My lawyer.

STATE'S ATTORNEY: Can you tell me anything about this woman at all? Are you afraid of something?

UNDERCOVER WITNESS: I'm not supposed to say anything. That woman might hurt me.

STATE'S ATTORNEY: What are you afraid that she might do to you?

UNDERCOVER WITNESS: I can't say. Please don't ask me again about that lady.

STATE'S ATTORNEY: All right. There is no sense going any further here.

(Turning to the court reporter)

Please note that the witness has been advised by his attorney not to talk about this case. We're done here.

The Conclusion

Because of the corruption surrounding these proceedings, and not being able to entrust the government of Gary, Indiana, these homicidal proceedings has been brought to the attention of the CIA of Boston Massachusetts, which is currently conducting an investigation. The truth still remains a mystery at this time, due to the lack of evidence.

Jamie Jackson went on to graduate from high school and continued on to college where he received his Doctorates degree at the University of Chicago. He later became a well known Baptist minister and civil rights activist, who travels the United States practicing his preaching's to the world.

There was an investigation years ago on Mr. Jackson. It was a known fact that Jamie Jackson was an habitual liar, and he has accumulated a criminal record during his teen years. Since Mr. Jackson's history was in the dark for a certain period of his life, his testimony was not permissible in court.

To this day, the link that lay between the Cryps and the Crezchek family remains a silent mystery.

The Cryp gangsters could not be charged with any crimes. Therefore, no DNA tests were performed.

The Cryps are known to be very violent and disobedient hoodlums, but only to find out that there *is* good in them. They have been known to participate in events that benefit exploited and battered children and have had a very high rate of success.

Nina Colburn, the young woman who testified against Detective Bruder, had a relapse with drug usage.

Shortly after she reentered a rehab facility in California, she developed a close relationship with one of the therapists there. She has been clean for over thirteen years now.

Chief of Police, Marcus Debroy, resigned from the Gary police department. He could not be arrested for the key in the yellow envelope that was found in his desk, because the safety deposit box C-13 disappeared and could not be found.

Detective Art Bruder was offered a job with the CIA of Boston, Massachusetts. After the trial was dismissed, he immediately resigned from his job with the Gary officials and is now in charge of the crime scene investigations lab.

Pastor Francis Jackson took an earlier retirement from the church than expected. He moved to an undisclosed location to be protected from any harm that might transpire from the outcome of the murder trial.

He and Anthony Crezchek did keep in touch with each other quite frequently.

Sadly to say, he was stricken with a rare form of cancer in his male reproductive organs and suffered for months with this illness until he died.

After Pastor Jackson passed away there was a letter that was given to Anthony Crezchek anonymously. To this day the letter still remains a secret and is nowhere to be found.

The blue van that was used in the triple homicide was registered to the deceased wife of Pastor Francis Jackson.

Anthony Crezchek is now married and has two children. He has been through several different treatment programs for help with his childhood psychological trauma.

Some of his ritual habits have formed into a pattern that has been proven to be uncontrollable. Doctors have decided to use an experimental drug that manages to restrain the release of chemicals from the right side of his brain which has been the cause of the severe verbal and physical abusive damage.

One of his two children has been developing behavior problems and doctors are expecting the second child to follow in pattern.

His marriage has been very rocky because of the violent emotions which erupted from childhood! He now resides in the eastern part of Ohio.

Mr. Crezchek holds his head up high with much dignity along with self-respect. He has a positive constructive outlook on life. He earns peoples support so that he doesn't isolate and alienate himself from the human race.

Both all-white trials were rigged and corrupt evidence had been falsified against him in gross violation of all his humane rights. After been caught lying, they will merely fabricate more lies to cover up the lies already told.

There has been information given to the media about the hearings. The public people has sent numerous letters and petitions to the judges on Mr. Crezchek's behalf. Maybe this will break the suffocation isolated in this case.

It was later discovered that the accusations made against Anthony Crezchek were false. One of the witnesses who came forth stated that Anthony did not commit any of the horrendous murders and did not bring harm to any of his family members.

But due to the Crezchek files being closed and reopened on more than one occasional legality this information did not withstand any relevance or importance to the subject matter.

Bob Segally, the undercover officer in this case retired from the Griffith Police Department back in 1976. Mr. Segally lived in Griffith, a town near Gary, for most of his life and worked on the police force for 28 years. He worked as "Officer Friendly" at Griffith High School and became very popular with all the students. After retirement, he then moved to Demotte, Indiana, where he thought he would enjoy retirement with his wife.

Lo and behold, he was dragged back into this case. Yes, the Griffith police department was involved in this case years ago. Like any other political events they bought their legal status out of the Crezchek case which left them dormant.

Bob Segally, was not only the officer friendly in the department but was also the agent who followed the case closely. He wasn't found out until now that he was also an uncover agent with the FBI.

Officer Segally was brought in on the case when the Crezchek murders first occurred back in the 1970s. He was the only police officer to remain on the case through out the entire investigation and the only one who kept his silence.

About the Author

Dragica Lord grew up in Northwest Indiana. As a little girl, around the age of nine years old is when she actually began her writting adventures. It wasn't until later in life she realized that she was meant to pursue her writting career. She graduated from the College of Court Reporting in Hobart and worked with deaf students in college classrooms as a realtime reporter.

Dragica still resides in Northwest Indiana with her husband Kenny and her son, River, who has Down Syndrome! To learn more about Dragica Lord and to keep in contact please visit her webiste at: http://www.readdragicalord.com. And follow her on facebook.

I am who I am. I do what I do. I am me.

The Crezchek Files